4 Steps Back to Here

DUKE CHARLES

4 Steps Back to Here

A
CHUCK T. BENSON
NOVEL

Dedication:

I want to thank my friend, Dennis Hoffman, for taking this ride with me and providing inspiration and encouragement all along the way. It was a fun trip.

Very Truly,

Duke.

Prologue

At the age of 77, I was newly widowed and recently retired. I sold my home and everything inside, purchased a new Cadillac SUV (the extra-long one) and a 30-foot Airstream trailer, and decided to see how much of the country I could travel before my aching, maturing body completely gave out on me.

I signed all my affairs over to my only child, my daughter, Lisa, in Midland, Texas, and loaded my ten-month-old, guitar-strumming labradoodle, Watson, in the truck (truck? SUV? semantics) and hit the road.

Almost 50 years of traveling from Corpus Christi to Waco up and down I-35 with every small town in between, working as a freelance, forensic scientist for small police departments that couldn't afford a full-time medical examiner and investigator, kept me away from home more than I would have liked, but it also made me a very wealthy old man with no one left with whom to enjoy my spoils.

Oh yeah, did I mention that I started writing mystery novels after Becky, my wife of more than 50 years, died last year to keep my mind from crashing altogether? I have already published four novels and have been working on the fifth one for about a year and a half and having a tough time finishing it due to writer's block, or maybe I just stopped caring. I guess we'll see. Anyway, my publisher sets me up for one or two book signings and speaking engagements every month, and I usually pull in eleven to twelve-hundred bucks in cash at each, so I guess I shouldn't complain. However, lately, I've had this fire in my gut that is not burning for the written word.

Chapter 1

I woke up in a trailer camp in Kerrville, Texas, to the sound of Watson growling. I opened my eyes, and it was still dark both outside and in.

I reached under my pillow, retrieved my cell phone, and hit the button that lit up the screen; the time was 6:11am,

"What is it boy? You want to go out?"

I started to get up, and my eyes focused enough to realize that Watson was staring hard straight at me, and he growled even louder as I began to extract myself from the bed.

"Watson! What's going on, kiddo?" and he moaned as if to say,

I don't know, and I don't understand.

I reached my hand out to let him sniff, not really wanting to get bit this early in the day.

I held it three or four inches away from his muzzle and waited. After several seconds, he inched closer until he finally put his nose against the palm of my hand; after he had smelled it thoroughly, he began to lick with his big, black, lab tongue I knew so well, still moaning as he went.

"What is it, big fella?"

If only he could speak!

Eventually, he became comfortable enough with my scent that he climbed up on the queen-sized bed and found his spot up against my thigh. The heat that his body generated was incredible and truly felt good on this frosty winter morning.

I reached down to scratch his butt, and something felt wrong like my arm was stiff, not sore or aching, but more like my sagging, crepey, skin had developed some muscle tone underneath it, which made no sense to my still-foggy mind. I drew my hand back and ran it over my nearly bald pate, and I thought to myself, *What the hell?* as my finger stuck in a full head of hair.

How the hell is this possible? I must be dreaming!

I pinched the bicep of my right arm; it hurt like hell, and just like my left arm, there was muscle covered by youthful skin. I couldn't stand it any longer! I dropped my feet over the edge of the bed, and there they were: a couple of thighs that obviously belonged to a much younger man. I shook my head and closed my eyes to try and clear my thoughts, then reopened them, and my thighs still looked the same.

I lowered my feet onto the floor, expecting the neuropathy pain and numbness to kick in, but instead, I almost sprang off the floor on feet that hadn't felt that good in 35 years or more.

Lord! This has to be a dream!

I flipped on the light switch just inside the door to the bathroom and stood frozen before the mirror. I recognized the person who was looking back at me, but I hadn't seen him in an awfully long while.

What is going on?

Watson came through the door, sat in a heeling position at my right side, and moaned. I couldn't tell if he was expressing physical or mental suffering or sexual pleasure, but by that point, nothing would have surprised me.

I ran my hand through a very full head of salt and pepper hair, remembering the way it looked when I was around 40 or so. The bags under my eyes were almost imperceptible; all the crusty blemishes on my face were practically gone, and my eyebrows had begun to fill in. I pointed at myself in the mirror,

Come on, Chuck! Yer a damn scientist; you know this is impossible, right? Yeah, yeah, I know, but I can't seem to wake up from this crazy dream!

Later on, I sat at the small dinette table with a steaming cup of joe laced with Crown, holding a double-sided mirror, the kind that on one side, makes a person's reflection look like he or she is in the fun house at a carnival. It was one of the few things of my wife's I kept after she passed, and it made it much easier to see the hairs growing out of my ears and nose and made it easier to trim my goatee and mustache, which by the way, had gained some color overnight as well.

Watson laid at my feet, groaning from time to time, not completely satisfied with this whole situation.

Seven-thirty in the morning South Texas time must have been like 5:30 in the morning San Diego time. I picked up my cell and dialed a familiar number,

"Hello?" the groggy voice on the other end answered.

"Will! Hey, Will...are you awake?"

"Do I sound like I'm awake...and who the hell is this? Tell me you are at my front door, so I can come out and pop a cap in your ass!"

Wilson Spalding was as close to a best friend as I had. We got together once or twice a year for three or four days of golf, drinking binges, and large steaks and lobsters. We met in college in El Paso at UTEP and went our separate ways when we went to different medical schools but stayed in touch.

He became a remarkably successful dentist and businessman, and me . . .well you know.

"Hey, Will, how about some golf?"

"Golf? We just got together a month ago!"

"I know . . . I know, but this is important!"

"Hey, I'm pretty busy, ya know?"

"What the hell are you talking about?" I asked? "You've been retired for as long as I have, maybe longer, and yer kid runs everything!"

"Ok, ok! So, what's so important you have to call in the middle of the night?"

"I'm sorry," I said. "Did I wake Kay?"

"Nah . . . she's not here anymore."

I could tell from the tone of his voice that her absence wasn't a good thing.

"Ya wanna talk about it?"

"Not now; maybe over a Crown after I kick yer ass for a couple of grand!"

That would never happen, not even on his best day! I would let him win every third round or so, just to keep him coming back; besides, it was never about the golf or the money. It was more about two old geezers rehashing old times.

"I'll catch a plane right away!" he said.

"Hey, don't get in a hurry. I'm leaving Kerrville, but I'm driving; how about I pick you up at the airport tomorrow afternoon? Text me your flight number and arrival time."

"You got it, pard; drive safe! You want me to make room reservations?"

"Nope! I got it covered," I said and pushed *End* on my cell phone.

"Watson, outside and take care of yer business! Road trip!"

I pointed towards the door, and he responded with a deep bark that shook the trailer.

I tidied up, made the bed, and stowed everything for the road. Then I backed the truck up and secured the hitch and safety chains.

Thirty minutes later, we pulled onto I-10 headed west for Tucson, Arizona, at a casual

76 mph. Watson was riding in the big, ol' overstuffed, captain's chair with his front feet on the dash and his head out the passenger's window, his tongue flapping in the wind. Did you ever wonder why dogs hate it when we blow in their faces but love to have a 76 mile an hour wind hit them head on? Maybe it's our breath? Who knows?

Chapter 2

Four hundred eighty nine miles, six hours and thirty minutes later, we arrived in downtown El Paso, the gateway to Mexico.

It definitely was not quite the selling point it used to be when I was in school. Time was, a person could get anything that was wanted and have a grand ol' time in Juarez, but now, about all a person would get over there is dead, so Watson and I pushed on.

I decided to see if one of my old favorite restaurants was still open on the far west side of town as I had a real hankering for tacos, and sure enough, there it was! I pulled into the parking lot of the *Riv* (The Riviera) restaurant, which in my opinion, was the best authentic Mexican food anywhere, or at least it used to be some 55 years ago.

What the hell was I thinking? The lot was almost empty due to the time of day, and the old sign caught my eye: *The Best Since 1937!* Ok, well, I'd be the judge of that.

I left the window down for Watson, knowing no one was going to mess with the rig with him there.

"Stay, boy! I'll bring you an enchilada or a bean burrito."

I walked up to the heavy wooden doors, which were probably the same ones from my school days and caught my reflection in one of the windows: WOW! I had managed to overlook my new visage for the past several hours, but then all of a sudden, my image in the glass made the impossible come rushing back to me and reminded me why I was even in this part of the country in the first place. Now, that's scary! I don't care who you are!

The smell of roasting Hatch chili and true Mexican spices filled the air as opposed to the Tex-Mex crap from the other part of Texas.

I walked in, surveyed the patrons, or lack thereof, and chose a table near the window where I could look out, and about then, the waitress came ambling over,

"Hello, you are new," an extremely cute and shapely, light-skinned Mexican gal said as she laid a menu in front of me.

"When was the last time the menu was changed?" I asked.

"As far as I know, never," she replied.

"Then I don't need a menu. I'll have three beef tacos and a small bowl of chili Verde, oh, and a Corona Michelada."

"When was the last time you were here, stranger?" she asked.

"Umm . . . I believe it was 1962," I said.

She gave me a sideways glance,

"You want to rethink that?"

"What do you mean?" I asked.

"Well, I'm a pretty good judge of age, and I'd say you weren't even born till at least the mid-70s."

Damn! I hadn't even thought about that!

"Ah . . . I'm sorry . . . what was the question?" I asked, "My mind was somewhere else."

"When was the last time you were here?"

"Oh, yeah, it's been 20 years or more," and she smiled, turned, and walked back towards the kitchen.

"I'll grab yer beer, hun."

15

The food was every bit as good as I remembered. I ordered a couple of hamburger patties and fries to go for Watson, and when she brought the bill, across the back in beautiful script was written:

Thank you, stranger! Call me! Carol, 566-6878.

I thought to myself,

What the hell is that about forgetting for a moment about my new appearance?

I walked out the double doors and stepped down one step to the partially blacktop-covered, caliche parking lot, which looked like it hadn't been upgraded since way before the last time I was there.

On the way to my rig, I passed by a mid-'90s Chevy pickup, and all of a sudden things seemed off,

"*Hola, Amigo*...where are you going?" said in broken English, a heavy-set, Hispanic man who was carrying a 100 pounds or more of bean fat with a sparse, black beard that hung down to the middle of his ample chest.

I looked around and noticed a smaller man, also Hispanic, standing just behind him.

"Howdy, boys, just heading for my rig to get back on the road; how y'all doin' today?" I asked with a certain amount of caution.

"Oh, we're doin just fine, *señior,*" came the reply with a heavy Spanish accent.

"Is that your truck and trailer parked over there?"

I was sure it was a rhetorical question.

"Yeah! Actually, it's my home."

"It's very nice," the big one said, "Why don't you hand me the keys, so I can have a good look at it?"

"Well, I'd be happy to, except the keys are in the ignition. I forgot them because I was in such a hurry to get some of this great food! Yer welcome to take a look, though, if ya want; it's open."

"Why don't you stay here and talk with Miguel for a minute!"

"Sure, why not?" I said doing my best to hide the smile that was forming on my face.

Now, Watson is the friendliest dog in the world except when he knows someone is messing with his property, then God help the person who is dumb enough to do it!

The big Hispanic didn't even bother to check; he just opened the door of my SUV and slid down into the driver's seat, and that's when all hell broke loose. The screams could be heard from more than 100 yards away.

Miguel looked at me with panic in his eyes as he reached in his pocket for what I assumed was either a gun or a knife, which triggered something deep in me, and I just reacted.

I spun halfway around, and the heel of my right foot connected with flesh and bone around Miguel's left eye, and he was out on his feet. As he began to crumble, I regained my balance and placed a perfectly executed front kick to the exposed crotch of the fading Miguel, and he crashed to the dusty parking lot, face-down beside their rusted-out old truck.

I strolled slowly toward my Cadi; no sense spoiling Watson's fun as the screams grew even more intense,

"*Madre de Dios!* Please! HELP ME! He's keeling me! Please, Father in Heaven, make heem STOP!"

By the time I reached the door of my SUV, the big man was half out the door, his right arm was caught between the bucket seats, and Watson was standing behind the driver's side with the bloody wrist and hand clamped tightly in his large mouth.

"Hey, Pancho! So, whaddya think of the rig? Purdy nice, right? Wait till ya see what's waiting for you in the trailer: it's Watson's big brother! Quit messin around, and come on, let me show ya!"

"Oh, please, *señior* . . . no, please . . . make heem let go of my arm! PLEASE!"

"So you don't want the rest of the tour, then?"

"No, sir! Please, just let me go!"

"Well, then, do you think we should call the sheriff or what?"

"No, sir! I don't think we need to do anything like that."

That threat turned out to be unnecessary as my new admirer, Carol, had watched me leave the restaurant, seen the two men approach me in the parking lot, and fearing for my safety, had dialed 911; the sirens were just audible enough to be heard over the poor bastard's cries.

"Sorry, pard, but I guess this just isn't yer day!"

After explaining the situation to the local peacekeepers and making a few more minutes of small talk with Carol who made me promise to call if I ever got back her way, I presented Watson his dinner, and we hit the road for our four-hour trek onward to Tucson, Arizona.

Chapter 3

Gary Moore was the head golf pro at Green Valley Patriot Golf Club, one of the best courses in the valley of the sun and the one on which Will and I preferred to play. I called Gary to give him my ETA and to let him know that I was pulling a trailer, and he offered to let me park out behind the pro shop as there were electricity, water, and sewage hookups, just like home.

I about had the trailer hooked up and leveled when Gary came up behind me, and when I turned, his face was white as if he were staring at a ghost,

"What the hell? Chuck? Is that you?"

"Yeah! boogidy-boogidy!"

I stuck my thumbs beside my ears and wiggled my fingers.

"What the hell happened to you? You look kinda . . . different."

"Oh, just a $180,000 worth of plastic surgery," my reply just seemed like the easiest way to explain my fresh look as I couldn't even begin to explain it.

"Nice job!" Gary said, still shaking his head in disbelief, "You'll have to give me the doc's name when the time comes."

"I'll be happy to, but you've still got another 20 years or so, before you have to start worrying about that. How 'bout I buy ya a steak and some Crown to repay ya for yer kindness?"

"Sounds good to me!" Gary replied.

"Momma and the girls are playin' Bunco tonight, so I've got a kitchen pass; let me go tell my assistant I'm leaving, and I'll meetcha out front."

"See ya in a couple of minutes," I said.

I checked out the trailer and put down Watson's water bowl and some dry food for him to snack on.

"Keep an eye on things, buddy," and he barked a low soft reply.

Gary and I headed south towards the Mexican border to one of my favorite steakhouses in the whole world: the Long

Branch, which had some pretty-dang good whiskey as well!

We ate and drank and made small talk until around ten when the chef heard my voice and came out to say *Hi*. When I told him about Watson, he went back to the kitchen and returned with a butcher paper-wrapped package full of prime rib bones just for him.

Watson and I managed to sleep until about 8:45 the next morning, which was sleeping in for us. We're usually up with the chickens at the crack of dawn; must have been the pounds of meat laying on my gut and the full ration of Crown Royal Reserve floating around in my brain. I had just stepped out of the shower when my phone vibrated, showing I had a text message from Will:

Arrive Tucson International . . . 1:30 . . . Southwest #427

I replied:

See ya out front . . . new silver Escalade.

He replied: *K*.

Watson and I boo-booed around and had some breakfast, or at least Watson did. I had coffee and a little fruit as I figured I needed to look after my new *svelte* body. Then we got a golf cart and loaded my sticks and went to the practice tee for an hour and a half or so.

It didn't dawn on me that my new, in-shape frame did not require the practice that the ol' Chuck Benson did; however, I did come to realize that the *new Chuck* had regained the extra 25 or 30 yards a club that ol' Chuck had gradually lost over the years. I kept finding several benefits that had gone away slowly with old age, and I just needed to adjust my mind to the changes.

I hit some wedges and worked my way through every club in my bag until I was sure just how far my normal shot with each club would carry. Watson sat just behind the ropes and would give me a bark of approval each time I purred a shot. I putted for about 20 minutes as Watson took a sunbath with all fours pointed towards heaven just off the putting green in the warm Arizona sunshine, and then it was time to head to town.

We pulled into the Tucson International Airport right at 1:30pm, knowing it would take another 20 minutes to get to the Southwest terminal as it was one of the busiest in the country, and it would take Will at least that long to collect his bag and clubs, and I was right.

I found a spot right in front of the baggage claim just as a very tall and well-dressed black man was pushing a cart with Will's clubs and duffel out the electric doors with Will following close behind.

I tapped the horn a couple of times and hit the switch, and the back door of the big SUV began to swing open towards the ceiling.

"Hey, buddy!"

I heard Will holler as he tipped the young porter and closed the rear door.

"Get in the back, pard!" and Watson climbed over the console and found a comfortable spot on one of the second row bucket seats.

Just then, the front passenger's door opened, and Will jumped in and got his first look at the new me. I extended my hand, but all Will could do was jump back against the door.

"Holy shit! What the hell is going on here?"

"Whaddya mean?" I said with a straight face.

"Who the hell are you?"

"It's me, Will!"

"But you look 40 years younger . . . I don't understand!"

"Just sit back and relax while I get us out of this traffic jam," and I punched the big V-8, and tires squealed, horns honked, brakes bit the concrete, and I was pretty sure I saw some guy in my side mirror flip me the bird, but nevertheless, we were off.

Will's stare was still fixed on me when Watson stuck his cold nose and wet tongue in his left ear, and if my new appearance wasn't enough, the shock of a monster trying to lick his ear off just about put him over the edge.

"Son of a bitch . . . who the hell is this, now?"

"Just calm down, buddy, yer gonna stroke out on me!"

"You need to stop and get me a drink and tell me what the hell's going on, OK?"

"Take a look there in the bottom glove box."

Will pushed the button, and the door opened to expose a very large, brand-spanking new bottle of Crown Royal Reserve, and he twisted the cap and took a long, hard pull.

"Does your furry monster share in the sauce?" he asked.

"Not this time of day; besides, he's only a baby."

"Lord, help us all when he reaches his prime!" Will retorted.

"You hungry?" I asked.

"Yeah, I could eat a small sammich to tide me over till this evening."

I pulled into the Cracker Barrel on the side of the interstate and rolled down the windows about halfway, and we went inside.

"So just what the hell is going on?" Will asked.

"Okay, well . . . here goes . . . " I took a deep breath and exhaled.

"Watson woke me up yesterday before dawn. He was acting weird like he didn't know me. When I looked in the mirror, I didn't know me either. The transformation didn't come on slowly with some warning or with a couple of young, black hairs on my head, just BLAM! I looked in the mirror, and there it was, or there I was, or whatever, and now you know as much as I do."

We talked for an hour or more; then we made our way back to the club and got Will settled into our digs. We set up a couple of lawn chairs and a small table under the awning of the trailer and popped the top on another new bottle of Crown Reserve and a couple of ice-cold brews. I answered tons of questions while Will tried to figure out if he was dreaming or just getting a little more senile. Even though he was in really good shape, he was still 76 years old.

"And Kay?" I asked.

As it turned out, Will's third wife of 12 years who was about 25 years his junior, decided he was too damn ugly and old for a rich gal like her, so she gathered up as much of their expendable income as she could get her hands on and hit the road in her new Mercedes S550 or whatever. Two weeks later, she ended up driving head-on into an 82-year old lady in a '78 Oldsmobile station wagon at 2am. Kay was drunk, and the ol' gal was lost, and now they're both dead.

"I'm so sorry, Will. I had no idea you were even having problems," I said.

"Neither did I," he replied, "And damn, I really miss that car!"

I almost choked on a mouthful of Miller High Life.

"I had a ton of life insurance on her head, but I guess if she had to go, that's the way to do it," and he shrugged.

Will always did have a way of seeing the humor in things.

We were about halfway through our second beer and shot of Crown when Watson growled, and shortly thereafter, a Green Valley Sheriff's car pulled up and stopped directly in front of our chairs.

"Watson, stay!" I said, and he settled back down at my feet.

Will and I had met Jeff Ray on the golf course in Green Valley about eight or nine years ago and became fast friends, and each time we came to the valley, he made plans to join us for golf, charred meat, and distilled beverages.

"Hey, Will, how ya doin he asked?" as they shook hands.

Then he reached out his hand and shook mine and introduced himself. I shook it with an extra-firm grip and a straight face.

He turned back to Will.

"I'm lookin for Chuck . . . "

Will just kinda looked towards me and slightly nodded.

Sheriff Jeff looked back in my direction and then passed me trying to find the party he was in search of. Then he looked back at Will and once more got the nod; then the light went on,

"Chuck, is that you?" he asked with an odd look on his face.

"Jesus!" and he sort of wobbled for a second or two.

"Try to calm down, kiddo, and I'll walk ya through as much as I know."

I poured Sheriff Jeff an extra-stiff Crown, then tried to explain my situation to him in terms he'd understand, which was hard since I didn't really understand it myself. When he was about three-quarters of the way through his drink, he remembered why he was here in the first place.

"Oh, no, Chuck! You almost made me forget! Gary told me you were in town, and we're really swamped with investigations right now, and I was hopin you might take a look at a case I've got."

"Sure, Jeff, how can I help?"

"I would appreciate it if you would take a ride with me, if you don't mind?"

"Of course, Sheriff, anything you need!"

We went about a mile on the back road behind the club, then out into the desert another mile or so, on a dirt road.

We drove up to what looked like chaos.

"We found the body about an hour ago, and we are still waiting for the crime scene unit from Tucson to arrive," Jeff explained.

We stopped about 30 yards from the crime scene tape and walked back over a couple of sandy mounds, and there she was, a beautifully-shaped young woman, lying naked, face-down and hog tied with her arms and legs bound together behind her back with what looked to be a lightweight, brown, home extension cord with the male and female ends cut off.

The first thing I noticed was that her hands and feet had been surgically removed-what a shame-but no visible pools of blood.

"Has anyone moved the body?" I asked, and Jeff looked at the young patrolman who had been assigned to watch the crime scene; he shook his head to the negative.

I approached very carefully to ensure I wouldn't disturb any footprints in the soft sand. I reached down and lifted her beautiful head full of red hair and turned her face towards me.

"Jesus!" I said, completely surprised.

"What is it?" Jeff asked.

"Someone tried to cut her face off and did a really crappy job of it, too."

I thought the young, pimply-faced patrolman was going to lose every meal he'd eaten for the last week as he started retching,

"Walk away from my crime scene!" I yelled and pointed towards the desert beyond where he was standing.

"Hey, Jeff, any other cases in the area resembling this one?"

He shook his head,

"Not that I'm aware of but let me reach out to the surrounding departments and see what I can find out."

I walked around the area and stuck one of my business cards in the soft sand next to every footprint and scrape mark that looked like it might be associated with the case; fortunately, I always carry at least 50 cards with me at all times, just a habit from my days on the job, and old habits die hard.

I looked up over the sand dunes and saw the flashing reds and blues of the crime scene investigators hightailing it in our direction.

The head investigator was a knowledgeable young man and a fourth-year medical student paying his own way through college; we shook hands and became good friends almost at once.

He actually was familiar with my work over South Texas way, and he was interested in possibly following in my footsteps. I told him to call me if it looked like he was going to have time for dinner in the next few days, and we'd talk.

As it turned out, Rex Blew made time and couldn't wait to visit with me. He was about three months away from completing all his residencies. He had been doing his internship in a small hospital this side of Tucson at night and working for the County's crime scene team during the day; he was just about frazzled, "worn to a nub" as they say, and he had a very rare day off the next day from both jobs.

"Do you golf ?" I asked.

"Sure do," he said.

"Eat steak and seafood?"

"Absolutely!"

"Like Crown Royal Reserve?"

"Yep, love it!"

"Wow!" I said. "Ya know, if you'da answered *no* to any of those questions, you would have been out on yer butt!"

"Well, lucky me, then!" and we both laughed.

When Rex's team finished photographing the entire area, I gathered my cards that had all my particulars like my picture, my phone number, website information, and the name of

my recent books, and I placed them back in the
pocket of my windbreaker (you know, at a half
a penny a card, one can't be too frugal).

That evening at dinner, I ran back over the
day's findings with Will and told him that Rex
would be joining us on the course about ten.
With all the excitement, Will and I both had
almost forgotten about my predicament until
he piped up,

"So, any chance of you hookin' me up with
yer witch doctor?"

It almost went right over my head,

"Huh, what? Oh, very funny!" I replied.

"Well, Dr. Frankenstein, you may have
come up with a way to make us both very
wealthy."

"Uh, yeah . . . first of all . . . " I said, "We
are already both reasonably wealthy, and B, I
don't have a clue how this happened or how to
undo it!"

"Would you?"

"Would I, what?" I asked.

"Undo it, dummy!"

WOW! Now there's a question I hadn't
even considered. If I could reverse this crazy
thing, would I? I hadn't played a round of golf,

gone for a run, or spent the evening with a young lady . . . or . . . the possibilities were endless, and all the things that I had laid in my bed and fantasized about just four days earlier were now very doable. I wondered how my situation was going to play out.

"Oh, I don't know, Will; I really don't."

The next morning at a quarter to ten, Will and I pulled up to the putting green, and Rex and Sheriff Jeff were there all saddled up and ready to go. Rex walked over and shook Will's hand and then mine and thanked me for taking care of his green fees, which if the truth were known, I hadn't. Gary, the pro, had done the honors, but who's counting, right?

"Not a problem, my young friend, just try and relax and enjoy the day."

"Thanks! I truly will! Hope you won't mind if I take a couple of calls along the way? I'm expecting some news on that body from yesterday."

"No problem. I'm kinda interested to see what the results are," I said.

We were all in the middle of the third fairway, and Will and Jeff managed to keep up with us even though they were teeing off from the geezers' tee boxes; they were still having to swing out of their shoes, and I could see both of them fading rapidly. Then it dawned on me that we didn't normally play this fast. I had been having so much fun keeping up with Rex, that I plumb forgot.

"Let's pull over under that tree and take a break," I hollered at Rex, and I could see the relief on Will's face.

We had been laughing and passing the large bottle of Crown around, enjoying each other's company for less than two minutes when Rex's phone rang,

"Yeah? Ok! Good deal, keep me informed," he said and hung up.

"They identified that girl from yesterday: a 16 year-old who supposedly ran away from home in the Denver area about three weeks ago, but now we have a kidnaping/murder case on our hands."

"Hey, Rex, what do you suppose the reason for doing so much damage to the body could be?" I questioned although I already knew the answer.

"Well, I'm thinkin she knew her killer," Rex replied.

"Have you determined the cause of death?" I asked.

"Yeah, it was a small puncture wound behind her right ear that went deep into the brain and caused instant paralysis and then death."

"And yet, the body hadn't reached full *rig* (rigor mortis) when we found her, so the deed had to have been done within the Green Valley area or at least, close by."

"Yep, you are correct! If I were you, I would contact the Denver police and have them see if she broke up with a boyfriend or possibly, a girlfriend recently and find their location. I get the feeling this is a love affair gone bad."

Another three holes at a slower pace and then another break; we filled our large tumblers with more ice from the cooler, and of course, more Crown. Three more holes, and we were back at the clubhouse, and Jeff and Will had caught their second winds; Rex, on the other hand, was beginning to feel the results of burning the midnight oil and the damage Crown Royal Reserve could do to a young, ill-prepared body.

Chapter 4

Candy Lesh was a very nubile, 16 year old girl with firm breasts, a thin waist and hips that were meant for bearing children. She had beautiful, long, red hair and a peaches-and-cream skin complexion, all of which contributed to her air of vanity.

She discovered that she had lost the attraction to her not-so-good-looking boyfriend due his lack of ability to sexually satisfy her; he was very scrawny and odd-looking, so after four years with him, she found herself becoming attracted to her girlfriend, which caused her 18 year-old beau to be very insecure and downright upset.

Mark Russell (Pea, as his two friends called him because his head was smaller than most and wasn't keeping up with his long thin frame) and Marsha Dalton completed the threesome. However, Candy and Marsha were beginning to spend more time together and include Pea less and less.

Jealousy can play mind games and do great damage to a young man's psyche, so one warm spring afternoon, Pea convinced the girls to join him for beer on the river. He picked them up in his two year-old Nissan four-door sedan that his grandmother had bought him just because she loved him, which he hated, by the way.

Not the kind of car for a cool guy like me to have to drive around in, he thought to himself.

When he passed the turn to their favorite spot on the river, the girls in the backseat who were laughing and enjoying each other's company announced,

"Hey, Pea, you missed the turn!"

"I found a new place! Have another beer and SHUT UP!"

They couldn't see the anger and anguish on his face. He looked in the rearview mirror and saw them completely enjoying themselves and blurted out,

"And don't call me *PEA* anymore!"

The two girls stopped what they were doing for a couple of seconds then went right back to laughing; if Pea had known that they were petting and feeling places that he could have only dreamed of, he would have exploded.

The back nine went pretty much the same as the front, except Rex's game continued to go downhill due to exhaustion, I was sure. Sheriff Jeff said he'd catch up with us for dinner because he had to report back to his office and bring his officers up to date on the recent murder case in his jurisdiction.

We sent Rex into the trailer to grab a nap, and Will, Watson, and I sat out on our makeshift patio and drank and sang, and Watson and I played the guitar.

You're probably wondering about Watson's prowess at guitar picking? Well, let me explain . . . I'd had him for about a week, and he was about two months old at the time, and I was sitting on the edge of my bed, playing and singing an old three-chord country song, and Watson's ears perked up. He came and sat directly in front of me and moaned. I stopped playing.

"What is it, kiddo?" I asked.

He moaned once more and raised his right paw.

"What is it that you want, buddy?'

He reached his paw out closer to my guitar and moved it up and down several times. I wasn't sure I knew what I was seeing, but I held my axe closer to him and kept my left hand on the G-chord. Watson pulled his paw gently across the strings, his nails acting like picks and made a perfect, melodic sound.

Thirty minutes later, he was strumming in perfect rhythm; he just seemed to have a knack, or a gift, or maybe he's even a *child* prodigy, or maybe he just had an ear for music. Honestly, maybe it's more like I'm just a proud pup dad, and he, like me, enjoys country music. We'll probably never know, but I digress.

As the sun was starting to set, Rex came out of the trailer with his hair slicked back and his face all shiny from a good scrubbing.

"Damn, I guess I really needed that!" he said. "It's amazing what a couple of hours of sleep will do for you!"

"You want a drink?" I asked.

"I think I'll give these cobwebs a few minutes to clear and get a little food in my gut to absorb some of the alcohol from earlier."

"No problem, kiddo," I said. "We'll be leaving for dinner in a few minutes."

We sat at a table for four in one of the small private dining rooms. Harry, the manager for the evening, was aware that we wanted to be alone and kept the other three tables in the room empty. One of our favorite waitresses served us homemade bread sticks with fresh creamery butter and olive oil with whole, roasted, garlic cloves floating in it, the house specialty: steak soup, and of course, massive amounts of Crown Reserve.

We each had one of the best Caesar salads ever and a two-pound Porterhouse with a couple of large, grilled, lobster tails that were sliced into bite sized pieces and served on romaine leaves and then, BAM, we were finished.

I mentioned, "I don't know about you guys, but if I don't get to bed, I'm gonna have to park on the side of the road and catch a nap."

I paid the bill, left a $50 tip for the gal, and we were gone.

Now, I'm not sure exactly how much liquor consumption constitutes being legally drunk, but I'm fairly sure I was way past whatever it is. I guess I've just been lucky, but I've never been stopped for a DWI; at least I don't remember ever being stopped, but again semantics, right?

Sheriff Jeff had left the restaurant before us, and I figured he was probably not far behind keeping us safe from the state highway patrol. Rex, Will, and I were just about to call it a night and sleep in the truck when we made it back to the trailer. Watson was there waiting for us, barking and turning circles with anticipation. The scene was chaotic: our chairs and small table were tossed, and it looked like there were signs of blood on the AstroTurf patio mat.

"Watson! Come here, boy!"

I checked him over, and although he had blood on his chest and around his mouth, as far as I could see, it wasn't his. I checked the trailer, and no one had made it in that far; I decided it was just a simple attempt at a home burglary. Rex headed for his car in the parking lot, and Will, Watson, and I hit the sack.

The next morning at the crack of ten, Watson and I found some remnants of blood-soaked denim cloth that I had missed the night before, so I turned Watson loose on the scent, and he tracked it back about 50 yards before it disappeared where it looked like a vehicle must have been parked, its tracks mingled with hundreds of others and vanished.

"This is starting to look like a little more than just a good ol' boy who wanted yer guitar, buddy," I said to Watson, and he growled his agreement.

By the time we walked back to the trailer, Will had coffee made and had placed two giant cups on the small table under our cozy lanai.

"You ready for some golf?" I asked as I sipped my Crown-laced joe.

"I think I'm gonna settle for "Judge Judy" and a beer.

"Ok, suit yourself, but keep yer eyes open, and by the way, there's a gun in the drawer on my side of the bed," I said.

"Got it!" he said.

"Watson and I are gonna try and catch up with Jeff and maybe Rex and see if we can make any sense of that young girl's death."

"Go on, have fun. I'll be fine," Will said.

I took out my cell and searched for Jeff's number,

"Hey, Sheriff! It's Chuck; you have time for some lunch?"

He gave me the name of his favorite joint in Green Valley, and I knew the place.

"Great! See ya there!"

Chapter 5

The Gilded Jasmine was an Oriental joint that mostly the locals as well as the seniors frequented, and I kept forgetting that I looked like a young man compared to Jeff and Will.

I rolled down the two front windows of my SUV and instructed Watson to stay,

"I'll bring you a fortune cookie," and he barked low as if to say,

Yeah! I'd like that or some Peking Duck!

I wasn't quite sure which.

Hot tea, iced tea, or tea of any kind just didn't seem to cut it when you have run as much booze as I had over the dam.

"Hey, Jeff," I said as I reached out my hand then took my seat.

"I'll have a Coke and keep 'em coming, please!" I said to the very skinny, very homely young girl with buck teeth who I assumed was the owner's granddaughter or maybe, great-granddaughter because no one in his right mind would hire someone so homely unless he was getting ready to retire and wanted to run all the customers off, so he wouldn't have to bother with selling the place. He probably leased the space anyway, or knowing the Oriental culture, he probably owned the entire shopping center. I guess my cynical mind just worked that way, then I realized that I was thinking like a 77 year-old and not a young man of 40.

Well crap! My situation was really going to take some getting used to if it persisted. I wished I had a clue as to why the transformation came when it did. There had to be a reason, but my natural mind just couldn't fathom it, and so I figured I would just take advantage while I could.

"You think we should probably start slowin down?" Jeff asked as he took an extra-long gulp of his extremely sweet, extra-lemony tea, and I thought I saw his eyes close for just a second or two.

"Why? Have you got something better to do like maybe go to church, or I don't know, maybe help the older gals fold some quilts?"

"Lord, please help me!" Jeff said as he took another gulp of sweet tea.

He had been a widower for at least 10 years or maybe a little longer, I didn't exactly remember, and he probably got all the action he required being an *almost* celebrity in the valley and could sleep in his own bed at the end of each evening. I'd be surprised if his icebox held anything but cold beer as the local gals probably kept him *fed and bread.*

The little gal came back with my Coke, and I couldn't help but think *bless her heart.*

I looked up in her general direction as I ordered,

"I'll have a large bowl of hot and sour soup and a veggie egg roll, please."

Jeff ordered a Number 3 with egg drop soup, and she was gone again, thank goodness! Some people are just not good to look at for an extended length of time, or your eyes might cross and stay that way.

"Anything new on the case from yesterday, pard?" I asked.

"Yes, it looks like our little gal and her girlfriend and *their* boyfriend . . ."

"Wait! What?" I said.

"Yeah . . .well . . . we're still trying to sort it all out, but our vic was dating this guy from school, and then she kinda dumped him and started dating this other gal; then all three of them disappeared about three weeks ago."

"OH, CRAP!" I said a little louder than I meant to.

"What?" Jeff asked.

"Well, I have a feeling we will find another body somewhere between here and Denver. You might send a bulletin out to all the PDs on the main route between here and there to be on the lookout for . . . what's her name again?" I asked.

"Marsha Dalton," he replied.

"Right, good ol' Marsha! So, what's this boyfriend's name?"

"His name is Mark Russell, but it seems like he doesn't have many friends, just the two girls, and they called him "Pea" cause his head didn't seem to grow with the rest of his body, kinda small, if ya know what I mean? At least that's what Candy's mother said."

"Yeah, I got it, Jeff," and that got me to thinking.

I took out my cell and dialed Rex,

"Hey, Rex, how ya doin today, kiddo?"

"I'm fine, Chuck. Hey, thanks again for the wonderful day yesterday! I really needed to get away."

"Don't mention it; we enjoyed yer company!"

I ran my ideas by Rex, and Jeff listened closely as we talked. After four or five minutes, we concluded when I told Rex I'd catch up with him in about an hour and a half or so, and I hung up just as "sweet thang" delivered our lunch.

You know, the more I think about it, the more I realized she was cross-eyed, too. That poor girl just kept looking worse and worse.

"Sweet kid," Jeff said without raising his head up from his egg drop soup.

"Yeah . . . sweet."

"She's related to the owners," he said.

Yeah, no crap! I thought to myself.

"You want to join us for dinner tonight?" I asked.

"Sure, but only if you let me get the tab."

I noticed you didn't say, *buy.*"

He smiled, "You're purdy sharp, there, Chuck ol' boy!"

"Yeah, I've been doin this for a long, long time," I replied.

"You might want to look in the mirror, my friend," he said.

I was about halfway through my second glass of Coke, and I just couldn't stand it,

"Hey, sweetie . . . may I have a large glass of ice, a couple of lime wedges, and an ice-cold beer?"

"Yes; what kina beers you want?"

I guess that was the first time I'd heard her speak, and it was just exactly what I expected. I had a feeling she was asked to leave China. I'm sorry to keep ragging on this poor girl, but some things just don't fit.

"I don't care, darlin, just as long as it's ice-cold."

"I guess you can only ride that ol' hoss so far, right?" Chuck asked with a grin.

I assumed he was referring to my beverage.

"Yeah," I said as I pushed the remainder of my Coke aside and went back to work on my soup, which wasn't half bad, by the way.

An old man arrived with a bucket, a wine stand, and two bottles of beer that were iced down; he sat it beside me then stepped back and bowed, and I nodded in return. Then "sweet cheeks" showed up with a large shaker glass filled with ice from behind the bar and a small bowl with 8 or 10 slices of lime. She sat them down and then stood back with her grandpa or great-grandpa or whomever to see what I was going to do with that concoction.

I squeezed one lime into the glass, then threw the slices in and poured a generous amount of salt on top. Then I poured one-and-a-half beers over the ice and took a big drink before it foamed over onto the table, a good ol' Texas Michelada, and Lord, it went down easy, and my head quit pounding.

The old man looked at me and smiled, and I held my glass high and toasted him, and he and our server bowed at the same time.

As Jeff and I were leaving the restaurant, the old man was standing behind the bar with a large glass in his hand, which I assumed was a Michelada, and he raised his glass and laughed out loud.

I gave Watson his two fortune cookies, and we headed for Tucson to meet up with Rex.

"Why do you suppose this guy made such a mess of poor ol' Candy?" Rex asked me as we sat in his office.

"Well, I'm thinkin' he killed her from behind because he didn't want to look into her eyes while she died, probably because he still loved her. Then when he realized what he'd done, he panicked and removed her hands and feet to get rid of the prints, and the more he cut

53

the more he realized that he enjoyed it and then couldn't stop. I'm anxious to see what kinda condition Marsha's in when we locate her. Did you find any semen in Candy?" I asked.

"Yeah, we did."

"Could you tell if it was done postmortem?" I asked.

"I don't guess we bothered to check that."

"I really think you should; he may have enjoyed the act, and it could be the beginning of a string of crimes as he could be going from a horny teenager to a homicidal maniac in a short time. This guy's gonna need money, and I don't think he's the type to hold down a steady job. I would bet he will probably find another woman most likely, wealthy, coming out of a market or fancy store and grab her. I would bet money he's homeless, sleeping in his car or laying low in an abandoned building or someplace like that until he finds his next mark. I've encountered his type before.

"That makes sense, Chuck. Thanks for your input!"

"No problem! Will you keep me in the loop? I'm kinda interested in how this plays out."

"Sure will, Chuck!"

It was after five by the time Watson and I got back to our campsite. One of the assistant pros was sitting in a golf cart, keeping an eye on the place.

"Mr. Spalding is over at the men's lounge with the sheriff, and he said to join them when you are ready to eat.

"Thank ya, sir. I appreciate yer help," and I slipped him a $20 and told him that Watson had it, and that he could go. By the way, did I happen to mention that Wilson Spalding was the sole heir to an exceptionally large sporting goods fortune and was absolutely "rolling in the dough?"

There was a high-class pizza joint called Ol' West Pizza on the side of the interstate towards Tucson that looked like a giant Wigwam with a huge pair of longhorns over the door, about 20 feet across. Its claim to fame was taking a perfectly good filet mignon, slicing it very thin, and covering about five pounds of pizza dough with pesto, steak, and mozzarella cheese.

Well, you know it's got to be good, and I like pizza and love steak. I'm just not sure which one compliments which. They serve expensive wine and beer, and the older folks in the valley seem to enjoy it, and it was also only about a half a mile from the casino.

When we're in town, Will and I usually spend at least one evening seeing how fast we can throw a couple of grand at the Native Americans, and that night was no different.

I had one glass of wine to be polite; then I ordered two beers to wash the sweet, sugary, wine taste out of my mouth. I'm sure Sheriff Jeff thought he was being a good host ordering wine, but this good ol' Texas boy is just kinda set in his ways and way too far along to become a wine-sipper at this juncture.

Will and I said our goodbyes to the sheriff and decided we'd all meet for breakfast at the club and another round of golf in the morning. But before we parted ways, we decided to go kick some redskins' ass and relieve them of some of OUR money! Right! What a joke!

The slot machine has the worst odds of any game in the house; that's why there are so many of them in every casino you visit. Will and I were aware of that fact, but what the hell; it was something we could do together while we talked or gazed into outer space.

We wandered into a smaller room off the main casino that had a small sign in a moveable stand that read:

High-dollar Slot Players Only!

I guess they didn't want the general public to see just how much those fools were throwing away.

The well-dressed young man standing guard at the door nodded and said,

"Good to see you gentlemen again."

"Thanks, Gerald," (that's what his name tag said). You know, sometimes it's not so good to be recognized.

We found a bank of $10 slot machines, and I said to Will,

"As I recall, it's yer turn to pick."

"Eeny-meeny-miny-mo . . ."

"Really, Will?"

"You got a better way?" he asked.

"Well, since you put it that way . . . this one's calling out our names," I said.

I handed him my black Am-Ex card, and he ran a grand in credit onto the machine then returned it to me and repeated the process with his credit card, $2,000 at 30 bucks a pull, the *max* . . . always play the *max*!

"How many pulls is the max?"

"Fifty or more pulls, I guess; who cares anyway? It's something to do for a while."

Unlike the Native Americans in Texas, the ones in Arizona hadn't figured out how to work the system, so we were unable to have a cocktail while we were giving them a small fortune. Lose $30 . . . lose $30 . . . win $30, did ya ever notice how people who bet X number of credits and got that number back somehow considered it winning? May have something to do with the *new math* in school, nowadays. Win $60 . . . lose $30 . . . lose $30, and that's the way it went, slowly chipping away at our two grand. To tell you the truth, we weren't really too surprised as it wasn't our first rodeo.

Just about that time, my *thirsty* was really hanging out, and Will was in control of the *Max Bet* button, and oh, yeah, we were almost broke. I was watching the cute, young hostess trying to give away Cokes and iced tea to a bunch of alcoholics, and I turned around to the sound,

"Winner, winner, chicken dinner, $500!"

Will looked at me inquisitively.

I shrugged, "Let it ride."

We both knew that was a mistake, but what the hell.

"Iced tea, please?" I asked.

About two sips of that crap, and I knew that had been a bad choice. I put the mostly-full, clear 20 oz. plastic cup in the cup holder of the old lady three machines down who was putting one five-dollar credit at a time in her machine and taking a nap in between pulls. The next time I looked her way, she was sipping on my drink through my straw, and life was good.

"Hey . . . pard . . . gotta pee! Ya wanna take over and run this thing dry, so we can get the hell outta here and get a real drink?" Will asked.

"Sure," I said, knowing full well that it was futile at best.

I hit a few double so-called jackpots, bet $30, won $60, then lost a ton. I tried to hit the *Max Bet* button and nothing. I looked at the screen, and there was only $20 in credits, and I almost pushed spin; then I realized *always bet the max,* and I fiddled around in my pocket for my money clip, removed a ten spot, fed it to the "bandit" and pushed *Max Bet*.

I was looking down the aisle for Will when all the whistles and bells went crazy, not a normal jackpot. I turned, and what the hell, I had hit the *Progressive Jackpot*: $26,590! Well, crap! Now we would have to sign papers for the IRS. Really? I felt too old for that crap!

"Hey, buddy, what's all the excitement?" Will asked as he walked back into the room.

"Oh . . . just won enough to cause a small scene."

"How much?" he asked.

"Twenty-six and some change," I said.

"Hundred? We got our money back?"

"No . . . thousand; oh, and by the way . . . you owe me five bucks."

"For what?" he asked with a look of confusion on his face.

"We only had $20 left on the machine, so I had to put ten dollars of my hard-earned bread on top to get a full ride."

He started to reach for his wallet when he realized he had over 13K sitting in front of him, and he nudged my shoulder,

"Take it out of our winnings."

Twenty-five minutes later, the short-by-wide lady who distributed the cash arrived with our checks, and I tossed a hundred on her cart for her and the gal who kept us company while the transaction took place.

"Well . . . that was fun!" Will commented.

"Yeah . . . I guess; would be more fun if we could get a drink in this joint."

I gave Will a check for thirteen grand and a couple hundred cash, and we took the elevator up to the tenth floor to the bar that overlooked the reservation golf course during the day and had a good view of the lighted pool and tennis courts at night.

"If I were younger, I'd be down there taking advantage of all that talent," I casually mentioned to Will as we drank.

"What? You are younger, you goofball!"

Once again, my condition had completely slipped my mind. I took another slurp of my Crown on the rocks and felt a very firm but gentle hand on my shoulder.

"Hey, sweety, buy a girl a drink?"

I turned, and the most gorgeous piece of heaven I believe I'd ever seen was standing there in a very low-cut dress, staring into my eyes. I was pretty sure I saw her from the corner of my eye walking by the high-dollar slots room a time or two. No, wait! She was the iced tea gal with fresh makeup and *real* clothes on.

"Hey, pretty lady, pull up a stool; what's yer pleasure?" I asked. I was fairly sure I knew where this was going, but I decided to play along just for the hell of it.

We made small talk for a while, and when Will started making noises like he was ready to go, she said,

"Aww . . . do you really have to?"

"Can you give me a ride back to my trailer after a while?" I asked.

"Sure, love! I'd be happy to!"

I slid Will the keys, "See ya at the trailer!"

He winked and started to walk away.

"Hey . . . you still owe me five bucks!"

He stuck his thumb in the air as he went.

"There is a cute little motel across the freeway," she said as we walked through the parking lot to what turned out to be an almost new Audi A-8,

"Beautiful car!" I said.

"Thanks, got it in the divorce," she replied.

I couldn't help thinking that there was a lot of that going around, which made me think of Will.

As it turned out, she didn't want anything but some companionship, and I got the opportunity to try out my revived body, which performed magnificently, by the way. Ok, so I gave her $300 for being a good sport, and she seemed satisfied.

She dropped me off at my trailer, and Watson was waiting by the front door of the lodge on wheels and started doing circles when he recognized me.

"It's still early," she said.

"Well, then, can I offer you a Crown on the rocks?"

She smiled.

"Have you ever heard a dog play the guitar?" I asked.

She looked confused.

"Yer in for a treat!"

Chapter 6

The next morning about seven, maybe eight-thirty or so, Watson and I enjoyed the warm sunshine and a cup of hot joe laced with Crown. I heard Will stirring inside the trailer,

"You know, this is a pretty damn enjoyable way to live, no yard or flowers to tend, and everything ya need," he yelled from inside the trailer.

"Yeah, but you live at the back of your property, and yer son takes care of paying all the bills and..."

"I know, but the possibilities are endless! You can get laid in every town ya pass through and then just be on yer way."

"Will, my friend, when was the last time you got laid?"

The silence was deafening.

"Besides, it's purdy hard to get laid in yer trailer when ya have a 70-something man taking up most of the queen-sized bed."

"Well . . . we coulda had a threesome," he muttered, and I almost choked.

Hot, Crown-flavored coffee running out of your nose early in the morning is not good.

Later on, we sat in the Men's Grill and dined on fresh fruit and sweet rolls that the chef and his staff had made from scratch and drank terrific coffee from some exotic place in the world. Who gets to travel the world and sample and buy the best of coffees? I wonder if there's a guy who gets to do that with whisky?

Watson was laying at my feet; the clubhouse was a "pet-free" zone, but Gary, the pro, had declared Watson to be a *service* dog. He tied one of those cooling scarves with the club's logo all over it around Watson's neck, and since Gary had become very fond of him, Watson had the run of the entire facility.

We were in the middle of the fifth fairway when my cell rang,

"This is Chuck; yeah buddy, what's up?"

I listened intently as I processed the latest information on the case that was being fed to me, and it was good to stimulate the ol' melon once again.

Watson was standing in the middle of the bench seat on the golf cart watching me talk on the phone. As I paced back and forth, he moved his head from left to right and back again, tracking me,

"Wow! That's interesting, Rex. Let me think about this for a little while, and I'll get back to you, kiddo. Thanks!"

I looked at Will who was looking very intently at me from across the green,

"That was, Rex," I said.

"What?"

"Rex!" I said with considerably more volume.

"Oh, ok, then."

That's when it dawned on me that I hadn't seen my hearing aids since we left Texas. I thought if all my newfound youth went south, I would be in a hell of a mess, especially if my memory went along with it. Oh well, there was no sense in worrying about it at that juncture.

Mark "Pea" Russell was sitting and thinking on an old, wooden, work bench in a trashed-out, abandoned warehouse just off the interstate a little south of Green Valley; there were three abandoned buildings in a row, front

to rear, and the local police had quit patrolling the area on a daily basis, and they only drove by if someone called with a complaint.

Pea had managed to break into the one at the very back of the property; he smashed the old, rusted padlock on the big garage door with a rock about the size of a grapefruit and slid it open, which took every bit of his strength.

He looked over the 20,000 square-foot structure very carefully as he drove around inside the deserted building. The floor was covered in a light spray of sand, and he was able to slide around the poles in the middle of the floor, which was very entertaining.

He found two five-gallon water bottles that had been left behind in the office area, one full and the other about three-quarters full. He used the stale water to wash the dried blood from his hands, and as some of the bright-red mixture of water and Candy's blood trickled down his wrists, he caught a whiff, closed his eyes, and inhaled deep in ecstasy. He ran his tongue up his wrist, and the taste of blood set his innards on fire.

He asked himself, *Is it time to find another companion?*

No, *companion* wasn't the word he was looking for. He had no clue about what had happened to him over the last couple weeks, but he liked it; he felt strong, in control, and alive.

Pea disposed of his blood-soaked T-shirt and jeans that he'd been wearing for almost three weeks in a rusty 50-gallon drum and slipped into Candy's khaki shorts. They didn't fit too bad at the waist, but his long, skinny white legs looked like "out of bounds" markers, and her flannel shirt . . . well . . . the sleeves were three inches too short, so he rolled them up above his elbows, exposing skinny forearms that were inked with several expensive tattoos.

He added his navy-blue cap to the ensemble along with his rubber flip-flops and thought he looked cool, when in fact, he looked ridiculous although probably pretty normal for kids his age. The next thing he had to do was decide how to find his next "lady friend."

Just across the interstate was a strip center that had a Chinese takeout restaurant, his favorite, and a pizza joint. Between the funds that were left in Marsha's and Candy's pockets and purses, he had managed to gather a little over $30, so he wasn't going to go hungry although he was really in the mood for some

KFC, so he decided he would do some scouting around to see if he could find one.

On the access road towards Tucson, Pea saw the sign he had been looking for, and he turned into the parking lot then drove up to the drive-thru.

"Can I take your order please?"

"Yeah . . . hey . . . ah, can I have a large bucket of . . . umm . . . original recipe, just legs, thighs, and wings, none of them breasts, ok?"

"Sure, hun, that'll save ya some money, just $12 instead of $16; how 'bout that, luv?"

Why does this lady keep calling me hun *and* luv? *Can she see me, and is she attracted to me?*

Pea's mind was playing tricks on him. He pulled up to the window where an incredibly attractive, young woman took his $20 bill and gave him change. As she handed him his order, in a very low and sexy voice she said,

"I get off at nine if you'd like a to get a drink, doll face," and he blushed red and drove away.

In reality, the "incredibly attractive, young woman" was 50 or 60 pounds overweight and probably way over 40, wearing lots of pancake makeup to cover the hard lifelines on her face, and she hadn't called him anything but *sir*.

However, Pea heard what he heard, and he was smitten for the moment. He'd be waiting at nine o'clock for her to finish her shift. His heart was pounding, and he was very sexually aroused. To him it was the best-tasting chicken ever!

Chapter 7

It was around five o'clock in the evening, and there was a warm breeze blowing. Will, Watson, and I were sitting outside, drinking cold beer, and just staring off into space. I looked over at Will who had his eyes closed,

"What do ya wanna do this evening?" I asked, and Will just shrugged.

"Hey . . . remember that strip joint on the outskirts of town that we went to a few years back?" he asked, his face brightened a little at the question.

"Are you sure yer heart is up to that? As I recall, they had some purdy good *talent* there."

"Yeah, they sure did! Couldn't hurt to check it out and make sure it's still is up to par," he said.

"Are you sure you can stay awake long enough to get there?"

"Well, if I can't, I'll just sleep in the truck."

Around 7:00pm, we stopped by the Gilded Jasmine, and my new friend, Grandpa, spotted me coming through the door. He laughed out loud and bowed, and I partially bowed back.

"What's all that about?" Will asked.

"Just two old friends saying *hello.*"

About that time, "sweet thang" arrived at our table, and I thought Will was going to fall out of his chair when he looked up.

We ordered our drinks and then,

"What, I mean, who the hell is that?" Will asked.

"The granddaughter," I replied.

"She looks like she was strained through a sheet."

"Hey, be cool; she's a very nice young lady," I tried to say with a straight face.

"One Michelada fo you and Crown on woks fo you," and she sat our drinks in front of us.

The old man had prepared mine at the bar, and it was perfect. He came to our table and laughed out loud, and I noticed he only had a few teeth; he bowed, and I raised my glass in a salute.

Will looked on with intense amazement,

"Do you guys belong to a mutual admiration society, or have I missed something?"

Our waitress informed us, "Grandpa is cooking something special for you. He like you very much!"

I don't believe I had ever had a meal such as that. It was amazing, and our bill was only $25, and I left sweet thang a $25 tip.

"How much was all that?" Will asked.

"A hundred and a half," I replied.

"And worth every penny!" and he reached in his pocket and peeled four twenties off his roll and handed them to me, and I stuffed them in my jeans and never broke a smile.

TD's show club was just a short 15-minute drive towards Tucson, and it was only 8:45 in the evening and still kinda early, but I didn't want to lose Will, so we went in.

Something else I had noticed was that my sense of taste and smell was beginning to return. Apparently, two or three mini-strokes called transient ischemic attacks (TIAs) had destroyed some of my senses, but they were starting to return; unfortunately, the inside of TD's was not exactly the best place for that to have happened as the carpets were soaked with draft beer and watered-down cocktails, and God only knows what else, which gave off a particular odor that once smelled, would have a lasting effect on the memory.

The cover charge was a $100 to get into the gentlemen's lounge (*gentleman*, now, that's funny, I don't care who ya are!). I'm fairly certain, there wasn't a *gentleman* within three miles of that place in any direction, including Will and me. Now, it's not that Will and I didn't know how to be a gentlemen, it's that sometimes we just didn't care to be, and I guess this was just one of those times.

"A bottle of champagne, sweetheart?" the cutest little thing in southern Arizona asked.

"Sure!"

I knew the drill, and I threw a $100 bill on the table.

"How many glasses?"

"May as well bring four and a date for my friend, here."

Will was looking through the big window onto the stage as a half a dozen young and voluptuous ladies danced and climbed poles and did the splits in front of the guys sitting around the stage. Ever wonder how there could ever be so many different shapes and sizes and still all be perfect? It is a miracle!

We laid down $300 more for the *talent* in the private room and managed to sip a couple of swallows of the very poor bubbly; our *dates* on the other hand, were downing it like it was Dom Perignon Brut. I was glad I paid cash that night, or Lisa, my daughter, would have chewed my ass when she got my credit card bill with a $500 charge for drinks.

"Whaddaya say about a decent drink elsewhere?" Will asked.

"I am surprised you are not ready to hit the sack right about now," I said.

He shook his head, "Maybe yer new youthfulness is starting to rub off on me."

"Alrighty, the casino bar it is!"

We started towards the SUV and just before I reached the driver's side, I heard a voice say,

"Excuse me, sir . . ."

I turned to Will, "Get in the car," and I pushed the electronic door thingy in my pocket to unlock the vehicle.

"Sir?"

"Yes . . . what can I do for you?" I asked.

The stranger was an average-looking man of color, and I was unable to tell if he was Hispanic or Black in the dim light, and he didn't have an accent.

"What's on yer mind, friend?" I asked.

"Well, I'm a little down on my luck, and I was hoping you could help me out?"

"In what way?" I asked as I looked at his polished shoes that looked brand-new and his expensive and freshly-pressed pants.

"How much *help* are you wanting?" I asked.

"Oh . . . I don't know, maybe a couple of 100s."

It took me a couple of seconds to contain the laughter that was welling up inside.

"A couple of 100s, did you say?"

"Yeah, you know, just like you were throwing around inside the club."

Will had rolled down the driver's side window and was taking in all of this from less than 10 feet away.

"Hey, Chuck . . . do ya need yer gun?"

"No, thanks, I'm fine! Me and my new friend, here, were just about to part ways."

"HEY! ASSHOLE! You mean you are NOT going to help me out?"

"You're very perceptive, my friend; why don't you just move along, now?"

"Why don't I just kick yer ass and take what I want?" he retorted.

Somehow, I just knew it was going to come to that, and I took a step forward and put the heel of my right foot in his mouth, and I heard and felt teeth break, and he cried out in pain as he fell to the asphalt with his hands over his mouth.

"Any more questions?" and he waved his left hand in front of his face for me to leave.

The security guy was running in my direction as I slid into my seat,

"I saw it all, sir. Just go on, and I'll take care of this," and I gave him a salute, and we drove away.

Lesson Number One: never go to a girly bar with a credit card that has a large amount of credit available. Lesson Number Two: never carry a large amount of cash to a girly bar, and Lesson Number Three: if you are not going to follow numbers one and two, be very proficient in the mixed martial arts.

We settled in for a couple of good, stiff drinks at the bar on the first floor of the casino that had dollar slots at each stool. Will ended up winning about $800 with me only breaking even, and he slid me $300 and picked up the bar tab. What a life!

After our outing, we pulled up to my trailer, and a nice-looking Audi A-8 was parked off to the side and "Ms. Cleavage 2019" was sitting in one of my lounge chairs with Watson's chin in her lap.

"Wanna go get a drink?" she asked.

"You up for a threesome?" I asked as I nodded toward Will.

"Looks like four to me," as she cradled Watson's head in her hands. I had a feeling she wasn't kidding.

We laid in bed at the cute little motel. She had her head on my chest,

"Do you mind if I ask how old you are?"

"Around 40, why?"

"Well, that's kinda what I figured, but you seem a lot more *experienced* than that."

"That's funny; Will was saying the exact same thing earlier this evening."

"How do you two know each other?"

"We went to college together."

"What?" she looked at me in surprise.

"He's a really slow study."

The next morning, Will, Watson, and I sat in the Men's Grill and dined on oatmeal with cranberries and brown sugar and a big ol' dollop of fresh creamery butter, soft-poached eggs on toast and apple juice (not that I needed the fiber as my new body had become very regular, again). It looked like it was gonna be a beautiful day for a leisurely round of golf.

Chapter 8

Around nine in the evening just outside the KFC, a skinny dude with a small head and lanky body was waiting in the parking lot for the drive-thru lady to come out.

"Excuse me, uh . . . ma'am . . . do you still want that drink?"

Peggy Morton turned around in shock as she locked the door to the KFC; no one had asked her to go for a drink in 20 years or more.

"Do I know you?"

"It's Mark, Mark Russell."

"Oh . . . I do know you," she said. "You bought the big bucket with no breasts this afternoon."

Mark smiled in relief,

"Yes, ma'am . . . you told me you got off at nine."

"No, I didn't! You are crazy! Go away!"

"Hey, wait . . . what did I do?"

"Go play with your little friends!" and Peggy hopped into her small, 2001, Toyota pickup and locked the door.

"I'd like to, but they're all dead," Pea said to no one in particular as his eyes rolled back in his head, and he took a deep breath. Then he moved quickly to his running car, and without turning the lights on, he fell in behind Peggy on Desert Palm Drive.

He saw her go under the freeway and continue on, and he stayed back well out of sight so as to not attract any local police cruisers.

Four blocks down, she pulled across the two oncoming lanes and into the parking lot of an average-looking apartment complex. He watched as she went all the way to the back then turned right. Pea made the turn and sped up through the parking area so as to not lose her. As he turned the corner, he saw her get out of her vehicle and walk across the parking lot. He then pulled directly in front of her and knocked her to the ground with the driver's side fender of his Nissan.

As he got out and reached to help her up, she drove a car key deep into the flesh of his skinny right forearm.

Fire raged in Pea's eyes while he closed his fist and drove it into her jaw, and she slumped to the pavement, unconscious.

Pea opened his back door and tried to lift her, but he could hardly move the dead weight. How could such a small, young girl (at least in his mind) weigh so much? It just didn't make any sense. He finally wrestled her into his back seat and threw her purse onto the front seat, and they were off.

"Where do you want to go for that drink? I'm kinda new to the area."

There was no answer, but Pea didn't notice.

Peggy awoke sometime later, lying face-down on a dirty, wooden work bench; her jaw screamed with pain, and she had a throbbing headache. She had bruises on her arms, and she couldn't move her hands or legs. She realized she was naked and tried desperately to focus, but the pain in her head was too intense.

She couldn't see her very fat, heavy breasts, but she thought she might be bleeding from her nipples, and her thighs felt hot and wet. Had she had sex? It had been so long she really wasn't sure. She and her roommate messed around on occasion, but that was the extent of her physical encounters.

"Oh, Jesus!" she screamed as her fat buttocks felt like they were on fire.

Pea smacked her beautiful ass again as hard as he could with the flat side of the machete that he kept in his trunk to cut wood for campfires on the river at home, and she cried out loud a second time. The top edge of the machete was a saw, and it cut through bone extremely well in Pea's opinion.

Marsha and Candy could attest to the benefits of the big knife . . . well . . . not anymore, and he giggled and thought a $16.95 purchase at Walmart had been a worthwhile investment. He said to himself,

Everyone should carry one of these in their car; ya never know who yer gonna have to cut up, and he closed his eyes again and smiled.

Wait! What the hell is wrong with me?

"Hey, Chuck!" my cell rang just as I was about to tee off.

"Yeah, Jeff, what's up?" I asked.

"We've got another body; pretty sure it's Marsha Dalton; they found her over around Mexican Hat, just above the Navajo Indian Reservation. She was pretty cut up, and her hands and feet were found burnt in a campfire, but they're fairly sure it was her; the MO is so close, and we are just waiting on dental records.

"Damn, Jeff! That's a real shame, but I'm not surprised. I bet the perp is still in the area, and I'd bet my pension on it."

Will was about to swing at the little white sphere on the ground, and he stopped,

"You don't have a pension," he mouthed.

I shrugged.

We sat at the bar in the Men's Grill after the front nine.

"Ya wanna play some more? Yer not lookin too spry," I said.

"I am just feelin my age. I've got an appointment with my heart doctor tomorrow afternoon; got a flight out at 10 in the morning."

"I'll have ya there in plenty of time, and it might be time to cut back on the red meat and booze," I said.

"Yeah, and do what?"

"I don't know, maybe go to church?" and I thought Will was going to choke on a slurp of Crown.

"So what are YOU gonna do?" he asked.

"I'm not sure; I have a book signing in Phoenix next week; guess I'll just hang around here and see if I can give the sheriff a hand with this crazy bastard who is cutting all those local girls to pieces."

"If anybody can catch him, you'd be the one!" Will said.

The next morning at 9am sharp, I rolled up in front of the Southwest Airlines' check-in station and the same young man who had helped Will with his bags came running over,

"Hey, Mr. Spalding, welcome back sir!"

"You must be one hell of a tipper!" I said.

"I do alright; besides, what the hell else am I gonna do with my money, especially if I have to quit eating meat and drinking booze?"

Will hugged Watson around the neck, shook my hand, and walked away.

"Talk to ya in a couple of days!" I hollered, and he just stuck his thumb in the air.

Later on that same day, Sheriff Jeff and I were sitting in the Gilded Jasmine just finishing up our lunch when he got a call,

"Yeah? What? Where? Crap! We'll be right there!"

I said, "Let me guess . . . they found another body?"

"Yeah, out of town a mile or so; she was posed in the sitting position on a bus stop bench, making this one a little different."

We left the restaurant and climbed into Jeff's vehicle. Watson was in the back seat, and I held onto the *oh crap* handle on the passenger's side as Jeff drove like a bat out of hell with his red lights flashing and his siren blaring, putting the fear of God in all the elderly population of Green Valley who happened to be in sight of us. He weaved in and out of slow-moving traffic with his hand on the horn, just in case.

We drove down a block or so without any buildings, only sand dunes with cacti and high weeds, and in the middle of the block behind the sidewalk was a glassed-in bus stop. There was a cop car with its lights flashing and two officers standing by as Jeff broad slid to a stop,

"Wow!" I said as lifted the sheet covering the body and gazed at the over-weight woman's torso sitting on the bench.

Her hands and feet were missing, and her head was in her lap.

"What the hell do ya suppose this is all about, Chuck?" Jeff asked.

"He's starting to enjoy it more and more," I said, matter-of-factly.

"Well, damn it, Chuck! You need to catch this little prick before he starts to cause a panic in my town! These folks aren't used to this kind of excitement!"

I looked at him incredulously,

"Yer the law in these parts, Jeff!"

"Yeah, but I'm not trained for this kind of crap!" and I could tell good ol' Jeff was starting to lose it.

"I'll see what I can do, Sheriff."

Rex and his CSI team showed up about 30 minutes later, and just as we were getting the greetings out of the way, the sheriff walked over to him,

"Near as we can tell from the driver's license photo we pulled, it looks to be a gal named Peggy Morton. Her roommate reported that her truck was out back, but she never made it into the apartment last night. Shall we go take a look, Jeff?"

"Sure, why not?"

We pulled around back, and the midday sun reflected off something bright and shiny beside the front tire of an older, tan, Toyota pickup.

"Stop here, Jeff; don't screw with my crime scene. Give me a glove, will ya?"

I reached down and picked up a single key ring with two chrome keys, and one appeared to have blood smears on it.

"Damn, Chuck, you got a set of eyes on ya!"

A forty-something looking gal with bleached white hair and a short men's haircut, wearing black jeans and a silver chain from her middle belt loop to her back pocket, in a black hoodie under a black, leather, biker's jacket and scuffed up combat boots approached and started talking louder than necessary,

"Did ya find Peggy? What the hell's goin on around here?"

She continued to raise her voice,

"Where the hell's my Peggy?"

"Is this her?"

I showed her the photo we had. She looked at it, and her eyes widened and started tearing up.

"Ma'am, she's dead," I said softly looking straight into her face, and she turned as white as a sheet and lowered her head.

In an incredibly soft voice she asked,

"Who do you think could have done this?"

"We have a suspect, but we haven't made an arrest, yet. Can you tell us where Peggy worked?" I asked.

As she wiped a tear from her eye she said,

"Just on the other side of the freeway at the KFC; she was supposed to be home by 10:30. Do you think this means she won't be getting her raise and promotion?" she asked.

I looked at Jeff, and he just shrugged. Shock and grief can cause people to say and do some crazy things, sometimes.

Fifteen minutes later, we were in the small office at the KFC, reviewing drive-thru surveillance footage from the last couple of days. The machine was set to automatically erase itself every 48 hours, but thankfully, we got lucky.

"Hey, Jeff, look at this video from yesterday at 3:14pm; take a look at this kid!"

The camera was pointed directly at Pea's face from somewhere up above and picked up Peggy just inside the service window as well. The sound was muddled, and the picture was very grainy, but he was almost exactly what I expected.

"Look at the way this kid's eyes are rolling up in his head, like he's on something or like he's in ecstasy just being in Peggy's presence, and she's acting perfectly normal," I said.

"Yeah, she is doing nothing provocative at all that I can see," Jeff said.

"Can you ask the manager if there is any video of the parking lot from last night?"

An unbelievably cute gal somewhere in her early to mid-thirties with just a slight amount of fat on her hips and thighs and really shapely breasts came into the crowded little office. I could feel her body on the back of my neck as she reached around my head and typed in the password to reveal the other camera positions.

"What are you looking for, luv?" she asked in an exceptionally soft and sensual voice, and I got just the slightest whiff of crispy fried chicken, which was kind of an aphrodisiac. Can't remember the last time I really enjoyed a juicy thigh or breast, so I asked,

"Could I interest you in a steak this evening?" and she pressed even closer.

She reached behind my head and came back with a plain-white business card with her info on it with *KFC* in red lettering, and *Jeanie Simms, District Manager for the Southwest U.S., (915) 833-4848* in royal- blue lettering and laid it on the tiny desk in front of me.

"I get off at six; call me."

I nodded and handed her one of my cards in return.

"Hey, Jeff, take a look at this," and we watched Mark approach Peggy in the dimly lit parking lot, and then we watched her get into her truck and drive off in a huff with Pea following shortly behind with no headlights.

"Hmmm . . ." I said.

We took the video disk with us and said our *adieus* to the KFC folks. Jeanie winked and smiled as we left.

As the sheriff drove me back to my vehicle he spoke,

"I was gonna ask you to dinner tonight, but it looks like you already have plans."

"Yeah, something just came up," I said.

"Don't blame you a bit!" he said. "Have a good time. Maybe tomorrow night?"

"For sure!" I replied as I looked straight ahead.

At 6:10, (I didn't want to seem overly anxious) I let her phone ring three, then four times, then,

"Hello!" a very seductive voice came back,

"This is Jeanie; leave a message, and I'll call you back as soon as possible," then a beep.

"Ah . . . yeah . . . this is Chuck Benson; we met earlier today," I said a little off guard. "It's 6:10; call me back when you can. Thanks!"

I hung up, and before I could top off my Crown, my phone rang,

"This is Chuck,"

"Hey, handsome . . . what's on your mind?" she asked.

"Well . . . I'm hungry, for one thing."

"Ok, then . . . why don't you come pick me up, and we'll go eat. I'm at the Casino in room 723."

"Well, ok, then, I'm just down the street at the golf course. I'll be there in about 15."

"See ya, then," she said, and the line went dead.

It wasn't quite a blind date, but nearly about. I wondered where this was going and would I still smell fried chicken as I stood waiting for her to answer my knock on her door.

When the door to 723 opened, HOLY CRAP! There was not a sign of fat on the thighs of this beauty, or maybe it was the skin-tight Wranglers that hid what little there was, and I did not catch a whiff of fried chicken, which was almost disappointing until the subtle smell of her perfume entered my nostrils, which chased all the thoughts of chicken parts off into the distance.

She was wearing a loose, white, button up lacy shirt that was tied at her waist and opened down the front to the point that more than an ample amount of cleavage was exposed. I could tell she was wasn't wearing a bra, and her breasts looked full and perky.

Her jeans were tucked into custom-made western boots with her initials *JS* stitched on the top, and the package was complete. I don't remember her hair being blonde and styled the way it was then I realized that she had been wearing a red, western scarf tied around her head with very little hair showing at the restaurant.

"Can I pour you a drink, hun?"

"Why don't we wait until we get to the restaurant?"

I was starting to get a little intimidated, which never used to happen when I was a younger man. I could usually hold my own in just about any situation, but there was something about this beauty that was a little overwhelming.

"Yes...we need to eat," I said, *and let me gain control,* I thought to myself.

"Mr. Benson, great to see you, sir!"

"Thank you, Harold," I said.

"Just two this evening?"

"Yes, somewhere quiet, please."

"Absolutely! Follow me, please."

Jeanie started to say something just as the manager came to the table and reached out his hand,

"Chuck, good to see you, my friend," and he introduced himself to my date.

"Your usual to drink, Chuck?"

I nodded.

"And for the beautiful lady?"

"A double Crown on the rocks, please."

"Yes, ma'am! I'll be right back," and he was off.

"Who are you?" she asked as she stared hard into my eyes.

"Well . . . let me see, I'm a widower, a retired crime scene investigator and doctor from over around San Antonio, Texas, and I write mystery novels from time to time and have a dog that plays the guitar."

"Shut up!" she said.

"No, really!"

"Well, I have got to see that!"

"I think we can arrange that," I said.

We split a Caesar salad and a filet and lobster tail and washed it all down with a couple more glasses of Crown.

"What were you doing at the KFC today with the sheriff?" she asked.

"Just trying to help out an old friend, and you?"

"Well, when I got to the store today, they were short-handed, so I pitched in."

"So, you don't know Peggy?"

"Nope! Never met her! She apparently was a new hire and didn't work there the last time I was at the store about three months ago. It's a shame, though."

"I spoke with the other employees; she was kind of a loner."

"Do you have any leads?" she asked.

"Yeah, they have a theory as to who the killer is, but don't have a clue as to his whereabouts. There is a BOLO out for him in three counties, though."

"A BOLO?"

"*Be On the Look Out*. Past that, I really can't discuss the case any further."

"Oh, ok . . . that's cool."

"So, what now?" I asked and thought I'd let her lead the way.

"I can't wait to meet this guitar-playing dog!"

"Well, my dear, finish up, and we will head out."

Back at my trailer, I brought out two very full Yeti 30-ounce tumblers with ice and Crown Royal Reserve and then went back to retrieve my guitar while Watson and Jeanie continued to get acquainted.

After three songs, she asked,

"Have you considered taking this show on the road?"

"We are on the road, and we love it, by the way!"

"You guys are terrific!"

We were on our fourth song when she asked to use the restroom, and I followed her in to top off our drinks.

I heard the bathroom door shut. Then about five minutes later, I felt her hands slip around my waist. I turned to her, and she put her lovely face close to mine. As I started to speak, she kissed me on the lips, softly at first, then with more vigor. Next thing I knew, she slipped her tongue in and caressed the inside of my mouth. She pressed her body closer to mine, and I could feel her breasts heave and her heartbeat speed up, matching the beat of my own.

She turned and headed for my bedroom, taking my hand and pulling me with her. Then she closed the door behind her.

"I like your trailer," she said as we laid close together.

"Actually, it's our home. I sold everything off not too long ago, and Watson and I are kind of fancy free, just kinda go where the *honey-wind blows*."

She looked kind of confused,

"Where the *honey wind blows?"*

I looked down at her, "Glen Yarbrough?"

Then I remembered that she wasn't even born back in the sixties or seventies or most of the eighties.

"I'm sorry, who?" she asked.

"I was thinking of the Lime Lighters; it was my mother's favorite group, but no reason for you to know who they were."

"Ok," she said as her hand moved down my torso.

"Oh, my! A hard man is good to find," she purred, and I immediately thought of Mae West. *You ol' fart!*

An hour and a half later, she got up and dressed. It was close to 2am, and I was thoroughly enjoying the view. It was one of the best ever! I was definitely smitten.

"Do ya have any plans for tomorrow evening?" she asked.

"You mean tonight?" I said with a raised eyebrow and a grin. "Dinner with the sheriff, but yer welcome to join us if you don't get a better offer."

"I'm sure, I won't; can I let you know?"

"Sure," I said.

She waved as she left. I laid on my back and counted 1. . . 2. . . 3. . .4. . . 5. She poked her head back in the bedroom door,

"Ah, excuse me, miss . . . can I help you?"

She giggled a little,

"Yeah, is there a taxi stand around here?"

"Don't worry; we'll take you back, just give me a sec."

On our way back from dropping Jeanie off at the casino, Watson and I drove the access road along the Interstate and looked for Mark Russell's car or anything that seemed out of place. I saw a couple of vacant storefronts, a gas station that went belly up, a strip club with

weeds growing high all around the parking lot and in the flower beds along the walk and front door, and some large warehouses, at least three, maybe more. The lighting was bad, so it was difficult to tell.

"Watson . . . this looks like the perfect place for a young amateur killer to hole up; whaddaya think?"

Watson looked out the driver's side window then barked low in agreement. I memorized the address and headed back to camp to grab a few hours' shuteye. I wasn't going in there alone and get hacked to pieces by some young maniac, and I decided to leave Sheriff Jeff a text message.

Seven-thirty the next morning my phone rang, and I let it go to voicemail:

"Howdy . . . this is Chuck T. Benson! The reason I'm not answering is because Watson and I are doing something important, we're on the golf course, or I'm really hungover and have the pillow over my head. Leave a message, and I'll get back to you if I deem it important!" Beeeep!

"Chuck . . . this is Jeff; call me as soon as you wash the cobwebs from yer brain. This IS important!"

Damn! It sure doesn't take long to burn up a night in Arizona, I thought as I tried to swallow without choking on phlegm, and Watson groaned his agreement.

Chapter 9

It was three o'clock in the morning when Pea realized he had forgotten to check Peggy's purse. He dumped out the contents on the bloody, wooden, work bench and was disappointed by what he found, which was nothing but the normal objects one would expect to find in a lady's purse, a comb, some lipstick (obnoxious red), a disgusting fragrance of perfume from Mexico, some gum, about 40 cents in change and a half-dozen toothpicks still in cellophane wrapping.

He almost overlooked the zippered pocket hidden on the back side (he wasn't accustomed to going through purses). Holy crap! He found several folded up (six to be exact) 100-dollar bills, a couple of twenties, a five, and six ones. He didn't know where it came from and really didn't care.

See . . . now that's what I'm talkin about! he thought to himself.

As soon as I get a little rest I'm gettin out of this dump, and he moved back to the front seat of his car and reclined as far as the driver's seat would go and drifted off to sleep.

By 9am Jeff, Watson, and I had driven around the first two warehouses and determined that nothing had been disturbed, so we made our way to the third.

Watson barked, and we saw fresh tire tracks going in and out of the big sliding door, so we parked and walked the next 20 yards to the door. The rusty, old lock was broken and lying on the ground by the chain.

I pulled my Glock from my paddle holster. I had decided to bring it with me as something told me that it might be time, and even though I was retired, I was still licensed to carry in all 50 states.

We slipped through the 18-inch opening in the door, and I held my hand up. I caught a whiff of something that I had smelled too many times before in my life: blood and decomposing flesh.

"Jeff, you had better call for backup and get the CSI team out here; we have a crime scene. Be careful not to disturb anything."

"Got it!" he replied.

"Watson, stay!" and he sat.

We worked our way up the right side of the empty warehouse, staying close to the wall, and the stench got stronger.

"Hold it, Jeff!"

I saw a long work bench with a massive amount of blood, flesh, and bone particles on it that looked like someone had made a feeble attempt at cleaning but then quit for whatever reason, and I was sure I knew.

"Is that a foot?" Jeff asked with a start as he pointed under the wooden table.

I bent down, and sure enough,

"Yep! I'd say that's Ms. Piggy's, whoops, Ms. Peggy's since everyone else's has been accounted for, so far."

We carefully sorted through the contents of Peggy's purse that was lying open on the bench without disturbing anything.

"Hey, Jeff, you might want to call KFC and find out if she had been paid recently."

He looked at me like he wanted to question my methods but started to make the call.

107

"If you talk to Jeanie, ask her if she is going to join us tonight."

"Ok, thanks."

He looked at me, "Yeah, Chuck, she got paid for two weeks' work about three days ago, $600 and some change."

"Yeah, that's what I expected. I'm going to bet our perp here has moved onto better digs although I'm purdy sure he's still in the area, because the hunting is good."

"By the way, Jeanie said to tell ya she's in for tonight. What's that about?"

"Oh . . . I asked her to join us for dinner; you'll get a kick out of her."

Pea looked over the large amount of used clothes lying around,

Wow! Look at all this stuff! he thought to himself.

He picked a small shopping cart with wobbly wheels, but he hardly noticed how badly the cart moved around. *Good Willies*, that's what his grandpa always called it.

No sense buying new when all those old people were just dying to leave this good stuff right here.

He picked out a pair of almost new Wranglers, a couple of western shirts, a new cap (at least to him) and a pair of worn boots, all for just 26 bucks and some change.

Pea couldn't believe his good luck. He didn't realize that he didn't have any socks or underwear until he was back at his fancy motel room then decided he really didn't need `em anyway.

The motel he found was off of the Interstate and down a not-so-busy side street; he managed to sweet talk the cute gal at the desk to give him a room all the way at the back. He paid cash for a full week, $400, and stuffed the rest in his shorts' pocket.

Pea changed clothes, walked outside into the Arizona sunshine, and took a deep breath. He smelled flowers, ocean, and the sweet scent of young girls; it was too bad he couldn't smell the actual stench emanating from his unwashed body; he hadn't bathed for well over a week, and the odor from the butchering he had done had soaked into his pores.

Food! I need food, he thought.

He walked back to the office, and to the small public area where the "all you can eat" breakfast took place and looked it over, but everything was cleaned and put away. The same cute girl who had checked him in called to him,

"Ah . . . Mr. Russell, can I help you?"

Wow, she was so nice!

"Yeah, I was hopin' I could get a little somethun to eat, but I guess I'm too late."

"I think we may have a couple of sweet rolls and some coffee in the back if that will work?"

"Ah, sure! That'd be great!"

"Have a seat and let me see what I can find."

Everybody around this city is so damn nice! Pea thought to himself.

I'll probably just stay around here for a while.

He had absolutely no recollection of anything he had done or the trouble he might be in. He just wondered how much longer it was going to be until Candy showed up. It seemed like forever since he last saw her, and he missed her like crazy.

Rosa Rose was in her late 50s, and she worked at the motel part-time when the regular help called in sick or whatever; her hair was in deep need of a color and cut.

I got such beautiful blonde hair, why do I need to dye the roots gray?

She laughed at her own joke as she saw herself in the mirror when she walked by. She was a sloppy dresser at best, but the motel always had plenty of clean polo shirts with their logo on the left side.

Yep, it was a real classy place! Her Levis could use an oil change, and the cow poop could stand to be scraped from her boots, but other than that, she was just a good ol' gal, and Pea thought she was beautiful.

She sat a plastic platter of leftover sweet rolls on the table in front of him, and he thought he'd died and gone to heaven.

"Cream and sugar, hun?"

"Yes to both, please, luv."

"Sure, I'll be right back," and she caught a whiff of something very nasty.

Pea ate like a swarm of locusts was set loose in the room, and when Rosa returned with his cream and sugar, she was surprised to see only one pastry left on the tray.

"There are a few more in the back if you'd like to take them with you. We'll just toss them this afternoon."

"Yes, please. I'd like that!"

She returned with a plastic sack that held another half-dozen rolls.

"What time do you get off, ah . . . what's yer name?"

"Rosa . . . and I get off at 5:30."

"Well, thank you so much for being so kind, Rosa. I hope you have a wonderful day."

Pea walked back into his room at 10:15am, laid down on the bed, ate the rest of his bounty, then dozed off into a deep slumber where he saw visions of beautiful young girls and their body parts floating through the air.

After a few minutes, his eyes snapped wide open, and he was confused,

Where am I? What day is it? What time is it?

After a couple of minutes, his mind started to clear and things began to settle down,

Ok, ok, I have a date at 5:30.

He checked the time; it was 4:27. He looked in the mirror. He normally shaved only once or twice a week at home and had grown a very thin beard, but Mark thought,

I'm a good-looking man, and the long scraggly hairs seemed perfectly normal to him.

His long, dark-brown hair hung down over his forehead and across his eyes, and it just added to the strange changes that were rapidly taking place in his body and in his mind.

At 5:30pm, Pea was parked outside the motel office between an old green pickup and a newer Caddy, and he thought,

One of these days, I'm gonna have me one of those, and he kept one eye on the Caddy and the other on the office door.

Rosa stepped out of the door, and Pea started to get out of his car to greet her when a big, four-wheel drive Ram 2500 with mud on the tires and all along the running boards slid to a stop, and Rosa climbed in. The driver squealed rubber and drove right by Pea standing in the drive, the big side mirror almost touching his shoulder. Pea shouted with all his might,

"HEY, ROSA! I THOUGHT WE HAD A DATE!" and he ran to his car.

"How was yer day, Mom?" the big cowboy driving the Ram pickup asked.

"It was fine, dear, and how was yours?"

"Maggie dropped her foal, and he's healthy and up and running, and I sold a half a dozen head of our prime stock to that big meat market in Phoenix, so all in all, we had a purdy dang good day!"

"Oh, that's great, Sonny! Have I told you, lately, how proud I am of you takin' over? Yer doin such a wonderful job since your no-good, sorry-ass, father ran off!" and a tear came to her eye.

"I know you still miss him, Mom. It's alright."

Pea pulled to the side of the country road when he saw them make the turn onto the dirt trail and drive about a quarter of a mile to an old rundown ranch house.

He saw his Rosa and a very large, very tall cowboy step out of the truck.

He thought to himself,

He looks about my size.

Pea was beginning to see himself in a completely different light. He sat in his car and waited for dark.

Damn ! I wished I had some of my Rosa's pastries!

His mouth watered just thinking of them.

Just after dark, he made his way through the barbed-wire fence and down the hill; the alfalfa was waist-high, and every now and then, a grasshopper would fly up in his face, and he'd swing the machete with all his might, thinking he was taking down a very large cowboy.

He crouched down when he came to the end of the pasture, maybe 40 yards from the barn. There was a light on, and he heard sounds of someone working, maybe shoeing a horse or something stupid like that. At the side of the barn, he could hear a radio playing really low.

Country music? I like country music; my grandma listens to it all the time.

He closed his eyes, and foggy memories of his grandma filled his mind, and she was trying to tell him something, but what?

"Excuse me, sir!"

Pea stood in the doorway of the dilapidated barn, giving Sonny a start.

"What the . . . what can I do for you? You lost?" he asked.

"Not exactly, but I am out of gas. I was hoping I could buy a couple of gallons?"

Sonny looked hard at the skinny, strange-looking kid and dropped the hoof of the big mare he was working on,

"Yeah, I can help you out; ya got a can?"

"No, sorry."

"That's ok. I've got one here," and he moved to a 55-gallon drum with his back to Pea, and he began to fill a five-gallon plastic gas can with gas.

Pea snuck up behind Sonny and reached around and quickly cut his throat with the machete he had hidden down the back of his jeans. Then Pea backed out of the barn and made his way to the back door.

He slowly entered the creaky old house. Rosa heard the footfalls and hollered out,

"Sonny, is that you, hun?"

"Yes, ma'am, it truly is!"

When she entered the hallway, Pea ran towards her and knocked her out with the butt of his machete. He drug her unresponsive body out to where Sonny's truck was sitting, shoved her into the back seat, then he disappeared back into the barn.

Rosa was gagged and hogtied face-down across the backseat. Her jeans were down around her ankles, and her pubic region ached and was on fire; her motel shirt had been cut open, exposing her large breasts that were burning red-hot with pain; she got a whiff of that disgusting smell from earlier that morning. She wanted to vomit, but the dish towel tied tight over her mouth made it impossible.

Pea sat up high in the driver's seat of the big Ram truck, and he felt like he was 10 feet tall.

Now this is what a man like me should be driving, and he smiled to himself as he headed for town.

"So, Rosa, where do ya want to go for our first date?"

She squirmed and fought her restraints, but it was no use because Mark "Pea" Russell had become very proficient at tying the hogs.

Chapter 10

Jeff had been held up on a case, so it was almost nine o'clock in the evening by the time all of us headed toward the restaurant. The southern horizon was glowing a bright orange.

"Wow! Something's ablaze," I said.

"Yeah, nothing but farms and ranches out that way, so I'm betting some family lost their homestead."

Jeanie giggled when we pulled up in front of the big wigwam,

"I've driven past this place for years but never tried it."

"Well, you are in for a treat, little lady," Jeff said, just as serious as could be.

I looked at Jeanie and rolled my eyes.

After we were seated and the server brought our beverages, Jeanie looked over at me,

"Oh my gosh, this is amazing!" she exclaimed with a very large smile on her face, and she took a longer than average swallow of very expensive wine.

I, on the other hand, held my flask to the inside of my left bicep and took a long, hard pull while I feigned a cough.

It was close to 11pm, and we were finished eating and just sitting and visiting when Jeff got a call,

"They found a mutilated body in that fire we saw; I need to leave."

"If ya want some company (I looked at Jeanie, and she nodded yes) we're happy to join you, Jeff."

We were almost to the turnoff when I said, "Ah, crap!"

"What is it," Jeff asked.

"That's Pea's car!" and all my suspicions were confirmed.

The fire department was just finishing up, other patrol cars were on the scene, and the officers were beginning to run yellow crime-scene tape around the whole area.

Besides the two full-grown horses and the newborn colt that died in their stalls, there was another full-grown horse that was tied to a post lying on the ground of the work area with its neck at a funny angle and its head toward the sky. A little further in revealed the badly burned torso of Sonny Rose lying upon a metal work bench; his charred head, dissected arms, legs, hands, and feet were all in a pile on the dirt floor of the barn; they looked like they had been in a BBQ smoker for 8 or 10 hours.

"Seems like Pea is getting off on the dissection more than the actual murder itself. He's drifting deeper and deeper into a very dark place (I know that doesn't sound very *medically correct* but considering the folks I was talking to). Did you find anyone in the house?" I asked Jeff.

"No, it's empty, but I just got the info on the owners of this place: a Sonny and Rosa Rose; they had owned it free and clear for over 20 years, and they had a son, Sonny Jr., who'd be in his mid-twenties about now. Guess that was who we found in the barn?"

Jeanie had been sitting in Jeff's car, and she walked towards me as I came out of the smoldering barn with my handkerchief over my nose and mouth.

"Are you all right?" she asked.

"Yeah, I'm fine."

I told her about what we saw inside the barn; she turned a little pale, but all in all, she handled it very well.

I've seen this sort of thing over the years, and usually the perp could be defined as *psychotic*, slipping deeper and deeper into a place from which he would never return.

It was well after 2am by the time I dropped Jeanie off and got back to camp and a long hot shower. Watson sat just outside the shower door waiting for me.

Once in bed, he snuggled up close, his back to mine, and I drifted off to sleep, dreaming of serial killers from my past. I woke with a start to find Mark Pea Russell standing over me, holding a giant knife, just about to stab me in the chest. My eyes snapped open.

Just a dream I thought to myself, and I laid there in a pool of sweat.

I checked my phone, and it was 7:15am. Watson moaned.

"It's ok, boy, just a bad dream."

I sat at my small dinette table with a steaming hot cup of joe and listened to Watson devour his bowl of dry food, and I thought,

I should be hearing from the sheriff very soon. I'm afraid Mrs. Rose's body is about to be found.

I wondered if it was going to be Rosa or the wife of Sonny Jr. I wasn't sure, but I knew it was not gonna be good. I had no way of knowing that the young cowboy was gay, no spouse of any kind, and the Roses were unaware that Sonny Sr. had been involved in a head-on car crash earlier that evening, rendering him dead to the world.

Pea came out of the bathroom and saw Rose's naked torso propped up against the headboard; her head was laying up against her fat belly, and her arms and legs had been hacked to pieces at the joints and laid out on the bed, making her look like she was eight feet tall.

The blood-soaked bedspread was starting to stink from the coagulating fluid that had seeped deep into the worn-out mattress and pillows; there was blood on just about every inch of the walls, floor, and most of the ceiling.

"You don't take very good care of yourself," he said in a low, strange voice.

"I can't be around you if you can't do better than this; I'm just gonna have to leave you here on your own."

He couldn't make any sense of why he didn't have much money; he only got about $50 from the combined pockets of Sonny and Rosa, and he apparently didn't know to look for the $6,000 in cash that was smoldering in the ranch house just out of sight in the pantry. Country folks usually had a stash around for emergencies. The fact that he had paid over $400 for his motel room and only stayed two nights didn't compute. It was getting harder and harder for Pea to make any sense of things.

He sat in the front seat of the big truck soaking wet and dripping diluted, bloody water onto the leather seats and floorboard. Pea had taken his first shower in over nine days, but he did it with his clothes on and didn't realize the difference.

I'm really tired, he thought as he drove on into the city.

He came upon the entrance to a small city park and found a spot under a large oak tree in the early morning shade and fell fast asleep.

My phone rang, and it was Jeanie,

"Hey, cowboy . . . how ya doin this fine morning?"

"I'm doing great; how about you?"

"Sure doesn't take long to spend the night around here, does it?"

"No, it sure doesn't!" I replied.

"Hey, I was thinkin: I've got a couple of days off comin', and if you don't mind, I'd kinda like to tag along with you and see how this whole thing plays out."

I sat in silence for a couple of seconds.

"Are you there?" she asked.

"Yeah . . . yeah, I'm here. I was just trying to think of how much trouble you could get in if you stayed."

"What do ya mean, *trouble*? I'll have you to protect lil' ol' me," she said with that low sultry voice.

"Sure, why not?"

What could possibly go wrong? I thought to myself.

"Why don't you check out and come stay with Watson and me?"

My phone went dead, and there was a honk from just outside.

I wondered who that could be while Watson barked.

"The door's unlocked!" I hollered just as the front end of a large suitcase appeared in the doorway with Jeanie close behind.

"Coffee?" I asked.

"Absolutely! A little cream and sugar, if ya don't mind?"

"What would you have done if I had said *no*?" I asked.

"Well, I guess I would have just gotten on the freeway and headed for home."

"Do I even know where your home is, or did I just forget?" I asked.

"I don't think it ever came up; I live in El Paso, but I spend most of my time on the road."

"Well, make yourself at home; it might be a little crowded, but we've always got the patio, and the weather is fine."

My phone rang just as I received a text message from Jeff.

"What's up buddy?"

"Chuck, take a look at the photos I just sent you."

I opened the pics that came up,

"Oh crap! Let me guess, Rosa Rose?"

"Yeah, the maid found her about 15 minutes ago; she's a real mess, and she may not recover."

"Rosa?" I asked.

"No, you asshole, the maid!"

"The devil made me say that, I guess. What's the location, and we'll be right there."

Twelve minutes later, we were at the crime scene, and I saw Jeff losing his cookies all over the front of his shiny cruiser.

"Sorry, Chuck, I've never seen that much blood and guts in my life!"

"It's all right, Sheriff; why don't you sit down with Jeanie and Watson and take a break."

I put some disposable booties on over my loafers and went in. The scene was pure carnage. It seemed to me that ol' Pea was really starting to enjoy his work! The expression on Rosa's face was that of sheer panic and reasonably so. It looked like her head had been severed while she was still alive from the blood spatter and the mess. The scene was unorganized and made no sense, and it seemed purely animalistic and savage, not like the previous killings, which to me, showed that Pea had completely lost it altogether.

"Anyone ready for some breakfast?" I asked, and Jeff started to heave once again.

"I'll take that as a *no* from you, pard. Why don't you give me a call when y'all get finished up here; gonna go get some of that greasy corned beef hash over at the casino if ya need me," and Jeff turned away from me once again.

"That was an awful thing to do," Jeanie said.

"Yeah, I know, but when you work around this kind of inhumanity for as long as I have, you have to find a way to lighten things up whenever possible," I said.

"You want to tell me about it?" she asked.

"Why don't we wait until after we eat?" I replied, and Watson barked in agreement.

Chapter 11

Pea was cruising through the parking lot of the casino when he saw Jeanie and a strange man walking to the entrance. The woman looked familiar, but he couldn't place where he knew her from. He was downright perplexed, which made his head hurt; he wanted to call out to them, but they disappeared inside the casino before he could get stopped.

He remembered seeing a big silver SUV on some of the nights he kept watch on the trailer at the golf course. He drove up and down a couple of rows and yep, there it was.

He stopped in the middle of the driveway between two rows of parked cars, and two cars stopped behind him and started honking. He flipped them the bird as he walked to the rolled-down window of the SUV and stuck his head inside; from out of nowhere a giant head with hot breath and slashing teeth was in his face scaring the living hell out of him.

I know that damn dog! It's the one that bit me at the golf course, and the realization jarred him back to a certain amount of reality as he ran for the big Ram truck.

Forty-five minutes later as Jeanie and I started to get back into the Caddy, I stopped,

"What is it? she asked.

"Do you smell that?"

"Oh, Lord, what is that terrible odor?"

"It's death," I replied. "Mark Russell has been here."

I headed for the freeway with all the windows down to try and blow some of the stench out of my SUV before it settled into the upholstery. As I made a beeline back towards the trailer, I pushed the "hands free" talk button,

"Jeff? It's Chuck . . . say, do we know what kind of a vehicle was stolen from the Rose ranch the other night?"

"I'm not sure, why?" he asked.

"There's a big, white, Ram pickup that keeps popping up in my rearview. I saw it this morning when we left the motel, and it's behind me now on the interstate."

"The truck was a Ram 2500 4x4," the sheriff replied. "What's your location? I'll see if I can get a patrol car up behind you. Stay on the line, so I can guide them in."

"Whoever it was must have some ESP because he's gone, now!" I said.

"Damn . . . that would have been too easy!" the sheriff said. "I'll put a BOLO out on that truck, and maybe someone will see it again soon."

"My gut's telling me that he knows one or both of us, so I think this thing is close to coming to an end; keep yer eyes open, Jeff! This kid is just crazy enough to be sneaky smart!"

"Got it, Chuck! You, too, and stay close to the phone!"

To get our minds off of the impending danger, Jeanie and I drove into Tucson and decided to do a little shopping, so we looked into some second-hand shops. As it turned out, Jeanie liked antiques and was very knowledgeable about them. She would have enjoyed the hundreds of thousands of dollars' worth I disposed of when I sold my house in New Braunfels.

In the third shop we went in, Jeanie saw an old 1948 Martin guitar, and she wanted to buy it for me.

"Come on, hun . . . it's only fourteen grand: that's a hell of a deal from the looks of it. We can probably talk them down a little."

"I . . . ah . . . really appreciate it, kiddo, and if I had the room, I might consider it, but Watson and I are just about maxed out for living space at the moment," I said and Watson barked low as he sat by my right foot with very little tugging on his leash.

"He really is a good baby," Jeanie said as she bent down and hugged his neck, and he put his chin over her shoulder.

"Hey . . . don't you be stealing the affections of my dog away from me; you two are becoming quite an item."

"Yeah, he's a very special pup," she said.

"He feels the same way about you, too; I can tell."

Pea went through his pockets several times and could only come up with $163. He needed food, another place to stay, and probably fuel although, he hadn't really looked at the gas gauge, and he had no idea where all the money went.

He stopped at a nationally known sub shop and went through the drive, almost knocking the lights off the top of the cab; he got two All Americans with extra pickles and no *tamatas* (he hated them damn *tamatas*, and his gram wasn't here to make him eat `em), six bags of potato chips, and four large Cokes. He filled up all four cup holders with large Styrofoam cups and set out to find a place to sleep.

Down the highway towards Nogales, Mexico, he looked for a motel that people with cash stayed in when they made their way back and forth across the border, and he found one that had rooms with TVs for $34 a night. He took a single room for one night as he needed to be frugal. He remembered his grandpa using that word.

I sure would like to talk to him. I wonder where he is, and where the hell is Candy? Shouldn't she be here by now?

His mind began to fog over, and nothing made any sense. He locked himself in the tiny room, ate his some of his food, drank his Cokes, and slept. Then he awoke and ate some more.

133

*Who the hell am I supposed to meet
tonight?*

He couldn't focus, and he just couldn't
remember, so he laid back down on the extra-
clean bed and breathed deep into the pillow
while the TV blared.

"What would you like to do for dinner?" I
asked, and Jeanie replied,

"I'm pretty comfortable right where I'm at.
Why don't I go get a bucket of chicken and
some beer after a while?"

"Sounds good to me. I'm always up for
some fried *chicky,*" and Watson barked his
approval.

We sat on the patio and shared a Crown
Reserve on the rocks and made small talk.

"So where do you think this thing is
going?" she finally asked.

"I wish I knew; it's only gonna get worse;
this kid has completely lost his mind!"

"How does something like that happen to a
young man?" Jeanie asked.

"Well, insanity probably runs in his family,
and he's been on the verge for some time. The
breakup with Candy probably pushed him over
the edge."

Watson stood and growled lowly as he looked in all directions and then turned a couple of circles then laid back down between our feet.

"What's up, kiddo?" I asked as he groaned once more.

Pea saw the dog he hated stand with his young eyes from his hiding spot on the far side of the driving range, and he ducked down behind a dry tumble weed. He stayed face-down in the sand until he felt it was clear.

I know that lady, and I should be with her. Why is this happening? I need to talk with her, and that man, he's always around, and I'm getting very tired of seeing him.

Pea's eyes rolled back in his head, and his thoughts floated off to somewhere far away.

"I'm gonna go get the chicken!"

"Let me go with you," I said.

"No, I'll be fine."

"At least take Watson with you; it will make me feel better."

"But of course! Come on, Watson; let's take a ride," she said.

"Watson..." and he stopped in his tracks,

"Take care of her," and he barked his understanding.

Pea jumped in the Ram truck; he floored the gas pedal to keep from losing sight of the pretty blonde lady and bounced over a few sand dunes, almost losing control of the big truck as he made his way back to the paved road in pursuit. He hit the back side of the berm, and all four wheels left the ground, and sending him airborne for what seemed like forever.

He hit the blacktop, and all four tires grabbed the road and squealed; it was all he could do to keep the truck between the lines. He smiled, then looked up and saw that he was in the other lane, and an oncoming truck was flashing its lights, allowing little time to get back in the other lane, so Pea just closed his eyes and waited for the impact.

He heard the horn blare as the truck went by on his left; when he opened his eyes again, he saw the truck in his side mirror leave the road and go airborne, then hit the ground and begin to roll, kicking up sand and tearing desert landscaping as it went.

Pea smiled and thought to himself,
How cool!

He took the turn at the end of the golf course faster than he should have, and he almost rolled to the right, but he managed to recover once again.

You are one hell of a driver! he thought to himself and smiled.

He slid to a stop at the frontage road and looked both ways. He saw the pretty blonde lady's car about a 100 yards away, heading towards town. He pushed the gas pedal to the floor and cranked the steering wheel hard to the right; the truck wanted to jump out of control, but Pea hung on, and he was off in pursuit.

Jeanie had called ahead to the KFC and ordered a large bucket of all breasts, extra crispy, and a large side of potatoes and gravy, mainly because Chuck had mentioned that Watson loved "taters and gravy."

"Hey, girl . . . thought you'd be back home by now!" the lady at the window said.

"Had a couple of things come up in Tucson, so I extended my stay for a few days."

"Well, you be careful, and we'll see ya the next time you are through this way."

"Thanks, Lindsey; see ya soon."

Jeanie caught a glimpse of a big, white pickup truck out of her right eye, and it made the hair on the back of her neck stand up.

My cell phone rang, and I pressed the green button,

"Yeah . . . this is Chuck,"

"Hey, it's me!" and I heard Watson's low growl in the background.

"Jeanie? What's wrong?"

"It's that big, white truck; it's following me!"

"DAMN IT!"

How could this happen? I wondered to myself.

"Where are you?"

"I'm in the parking lot of the strip center where the liquor store is."

"Ok . . . don't stop, just keep driving around the lot and avoid him. I'm on my way. Don't hang up; I'm gonna call Jeff, and we'll be on a conference call with him."

We both heard the dial tone and then,

"Sheriff Ray . . ."

"Jeff . . . it's Chuck; Jeanie's at the liquor store in the strip center, and I think Pea has her in his sights!"

There was silence; then I heard tires squeal,

"I'm about three minutes away, Chuck."

"I'm just pulling out of the golf course; you be very careful; this guy is completely gone. If you get the chance, Jeff, put him down; that's the only way we're gonna stop him!"

"Ten-four . . . are you still there, Jeanie?"

"Yes . . . I'm here, but he's right behind me. I think he's . . ." BAM! Then there was only silence.

I ran the light and made the turn under the freeway and then again on the other side without causing a traffic accident, and I saw a car upside down in the grassy area between the parking lot of the liquor store and the access road.

Jeff's police vehicle was parked at an angle with its front wheels over the line in a parking space with the driver's door open. I saw him lying face down in the grass. I jumped the curb and went broad-sliding to a stop. Jeff's neck was cut, and the blood was pooling around his head.

I looked up just in time to see the big Ram highballing it south on the access road.

Watson was lying upside down on the roof of the car, which was now where the floor should be; lucky for me, the back door opened without any resistance, and I was able to drag him out. I checked him over quickly, and all I could find was a large bump behind his right eye. I carried him to the Caddy and laid him on the back seat then took off in pursuit of Mark Russell. The whole thing was going to end that night, no matter what!

I was doing 98 mph, and I could see cars up ahead with their brake lights flashing all the way across five lanes of the freeway like someone was swerving in and out of traffic at a high rate of speed.

I couldn't see him, but I could feel I was close, so I kept the "hammer" down; the speedometer read 104 mph, then 110; I turned on my emergency flashers, hoping that would give the traffic ahead some kind of warning, but at my speed, all it would take was a scared, little ol' man gigging when I needed him to jog, and we'd all be toast.

I was passing a VW bug on the right when I felt a cold, wet nose in my right ear,

"Hey, kiddo, how ya doin?" and Watson let out a bark that shook the entire truck.

"Candy . . . you finally made it!" Pea said in a strange, muffled voice, and he held the big blood-stained knife to Jeanie's throat as he tore in and out of slow-moving traffic.

Play along; if he thinks you really are Candy, he may not kill you quite so quickly, she thought to herself in desperation.

"Yes, Pea, I'm here, hun."

"I asked you not to call me Pea . . . I don't like it!"

He held the machete to her neck, and a quick turn caused it to cut a deep, but not fatal, gash in her neck, and she whimpered.

"Why don't you put the knife down, hun? We're together, now, and everything is gonna be fine!"

He relaxed his hand, and the machete moved down and rested across the top of her breasts.

The stench inside the truck was sickening, and it was all Jeanie could do to keep from vomiting. She remembered that Chuck said it was the smell of death. She had a feeling that once it got in her nostrils, she'd never get rid of it.

Pea sat up high and drove with his left hand. He wondered to himself,

Is this really Candy who's with me, and if so, why am I holding a knife on her, and where has she been all this time?

Pea hit another curb as he got off the freeway at his exit, and the blade of the big machete bit into the top of Jeanie's right breast, and she flinched as another stream of blood started down her body.

I won't let this little son of a bitch see me cry! I just won't! and she closed her eyes and forced the pain to go away.

I saw the stop lights of at least a dozen vehicles all come on at once, and I saw the big Ram cut across three lanes of traffic to make the exit; fortunately, I was back far enough and was able to get over without pissing too many people off. Watson stood with his front feet on the dash and barked loud,

"Yeah, kiddo...I see `em!" and we slid to a stop at the access road.

They were a couple hundred yards ahead of us, and there were big clouds of dust in the air from Pea's erratic driving. There was a dimly lit motel sign up ahead, and I thought I saw them pull off the road and into the parking area. I pulled over to use my phone,

"Nine-one-one, what's your emergency?"

"This is Dr. Chuck Benson, and I'm in pursuit of a murder suspect!"

"Yes, Dr. Benson, we've been trying to locate you; what's your situation?"

"We just left the freeway at Exit 12, and the suspect turned into the Sagebrush Motel, south on the access road a mile or so."

"Dr. Benson, you need to stay back and let the State Police handle this; do you copy?"

"Yes . . . I understand, but I'm afraid there's no time to do that! Y'all just need to hurry!" and I pulled slowly onto the dirt parking lot.

I saw the truck with smoke rolling out from under the hood parked at the very back.

Jeanie laid on a stinky bed on her back with her right hand on her neck and her left pressing down on her breast trying to stop the bleeding. Pea stood by the head of the bed with the machete in his right hand.

"Tell me again why you were gone so long!" he demanded.

"Oh, baby, it hasn't been so long. I just had to take care of those things we talked about, and it took a little longer than I planned."

Pea tried to understand, but something was wrong; he didn't know what, but there was definitely something not quite right.

Jeanie knew if she kept talking in generalities that she couldn't get into too much trouble as long as she could just keep him believing that she was Candy.

Pea looked at her with his crazy eyes and his hair hanging over and took a deep breath,

"Who are you? You don't smell like my Candy. Who the hell are you?" he screamed.

The Spanish music on the radio was playing so loud in the background that she could hardly hear him. He raised the machete high above his head, and Jeanie closed her eyes; she just knew this was the end.

Pea paused briefly as he got a glimpse of his . . . *grandpa?* All of a sudden, the door was crushed inward by the front end of a big Cadillac Escalade; Watson flew through the air in attack mode, but he was met by an off-handed blow from a big knife that went deep into his left shoulder. He fell to the ground in great pain but managed to limp the last yard or so and clamp his big mouth around the right ankle of his enemy.

I stepped out and slammed a round into the chamber of my Glock. Between Jeanie on the nasty bed and Watson biting hard on his leg, Pea was confused just long enough for me to fire two rounds. The first one hit him in the forehead, and the second hit him in the right eye, and I paused as he slumped.

Now, as a doctor and a medical examiner, I've seen thousands of gunshot wounds, and I was positive he was dead before he hit the floor, but for some unknown reason, I lifted my weapon and placed four more in his heart. Overkill, you ask? I don't know, but I thought,

If he wiggles, I have 9 more, and I'd be happy to let him take them with him on his journey to hell.

I went over to Jeanie who was still bleeding fairly good from her injuries and looked her over for any that might be life-threatening. Luckily, there were none, and I immediately called for an ambulance just in case one hadn't been dispatched.

"Are you all right, gal?"

"Yes, I'll live, but is Pea . . . dead?" she asked in a worried voice.

"Yah, don't worry; it's all over, now."

I went over to Watson and put my hand on his bleeding shoulder. When the ambulance finished loading Jeanie, I loaded Watson in the Caddy and followed the ambulance to the hospital.

An hour later, I was running between two separate ERs in a small hospital up the freeway about four miles towards Tucson. The doctor who was stitching up the inside of Watson's wound was a young intern and didn't have quite the necessary skills in my opinion, so I took over and had him go lend a hand with Jeanie's injuries.

I stapled the outside of Watson's wound and figured he'd be as good as new in a couple of weeks.

The ER staff weren't overly enthusiastic about having a canine in one of their rooms to which I said,

"That's ok because I assure you, he's not very happy about being here."

Chapter 12

The next morning, we all slept in.

Gary over at the golf shop had seen all the excitement on TV, and we had talked a couple of times throughout the night.

"Call me when you wake up, and I'll have breakfast sent over."

"Thanks, pard," I said.

"Mornin, gal; how ya feelin?"

"Like I've been shot at and hit! Did we eat last night because all I can remember is chicken breasts flying through the air and me trying to grab a bite as they went by."

"Speaking of breasts . . . how's that one of yers doin?"

"I'm not sure; wanna hold it . . . gently?" she added.

"What's yer pleasure, my lady?"

"I'm still waitin for you to hold my breast."

I bent down and ever so softly, kissed her just above her bandaged mound,

"I meant . . . what would you like for breakfast?"

"I don't care . . . definitely lots of coffee, though, and whatever else is fine with me."

It was 10:30 by the time we settled down on the patio, and one of the chefs drove up in a golf cart loaded down with juice, fresh pastries, sausage links, ham, thick-cut bacon, oven-cooked country potatoes with bell peppers and onions, eight or nine poached eggs, and a stack of English muffins with some really good preserves.

"WOW!" Jeanie said, "I think I'm in heaven. I could just sit right here from now on," and she closed her eyes and let her skin soak up the warm Arizona sun.

"Did I tell you I am a golfer?" she asked.

"I don't believe it came up," I said, "But I'm not surprised. What's yer handicap?"

"Normally a 10, but with this hole in my boob, I may need a couple more strokes."

"We may just need to give it a try next time around."

"You got a date, buster," and she laughed.

"So, who do we need to call about yer car? It was kinda trashed."

"It was a rental. I'll just call corporate, and they'll send out another one. Why . . . are you tryin' to get rid of me?" she asked.

"Nope, not at all! I'm just one who likes to tie up loose ends."

Back in Denver, Pea's grandma, Glenna Russell, cried for hours after she received the call that she knew had to be coming sooner or later; when the police finally left, she gathered her emotions, walked out to the old barn, and began digging through her dead husband's tools.

There were boxes and boxes of them; he could make or repair anything, and she knew exactly what she was looking for. After 30 minutes of moving tools from one spot to another, she had found what she was looking for; she had completely overlooked it as it was over in the corner, partially covered by some dried up ol' hay: *the hatchet*, the one she and her late husband had killed so many hundreds of chickens with over the years.

She retrieved it and sprayed it heavily with WD40 then set it on the old, wooden, work bench while she waited. At last, she fired up the old grinder and began to take the rust down to shiny metal; then she turned on the belt sander and began to polish the blade; then when it met her specifications, she went to work on the blade, honing the perfect edge that would cut through a man's gullet without any resistance, and Dr. Chuck T. Benson was just the man she was going to take down!

WHO IN THE HELL DOES HE THINK HE IS KILLING MY BABY?

The more she thought, the louder the noise in her head became.

Glenna had done her research; her poor computer skills caused her a little more trouble than she was used to, but she was determined and found Dr. Chuck T. Benson, Author and went to his webpage; on it, she found his calendar of speaking engagements and book signings. He was going to be in Denver in less than two weeks. *Perfect!*

She sanded the entire handle and brushed on a goodly amount of linseed oil like her husband had showed her all those years ago. Then she let the linseed oil soak in.

Just for looks, she took some leather strips and laced the grip; she always did like going that extra mile to make things look beautiful, like with her cakes, cookies, and all the meals she prepared lovingly for her men.

She was ready.

Chuck T. Benson.. . . . I am coming for YOU!

Chapter 13

We spent the day just soaking up the warm, Arizona sunshine, and I made a few calls to the Tucson Police Department to try and find out more information on Jeff's memorial service.

He had a son and a daughter; one would be flying in from northern California that evening, and the other would be coming from somewhere in Montana the next morning.

Rex Blew, my young friend from the Tucson CSI, called shortly after I settled back down in my chair with a couple of fresh tumblers of Crown and ice.

"Hey, Rex! What's up, kiddo?"

"Are you still in town? I'd like to stop by and pick your brain."

"Sure! I'm not certain there's much left, but yer welcome to whatever there is."

"Ok, great! I am about 15 minutes out!"

"Ok, we'll see you soon."

When he arrived, I poured him a small Crown on the rocks and told him to pull up a chair.

"You've been a busy guy, had us hopping for the last few days."

"Yeah, sorry," I said. "Not exactly how I planned on spending a few days off, but I guess beggars can't be choosers."

"So . . . how did you wind up tracking that psycho down?"

"Well . . . actually, he found us. All the other women he picked up were pretty much plain-Janes, but when he saw Jeanie here, he thought she was his girl, Candy. I'm still not sure where he first saw her, but anyway, I guess he had to get to her, and so the chase was on! We were just incredibly lucky everything turned out the way it did!"

We made small talk for a while then vowed to see each other at the memorial, and he was off.

Jeanie, Watson, and I enjoyed the setting sun, and I dozed off in my chair and fell into a dream-like state . . .

"Where are we headed?"

"To the airport."

I said, "I don't need to go to the airport; the company is having a car delivered."

My mind was kinda fuzzy.

"Are you feeling alright?" Jeanie asked.

"You're looking kinda strange: yer skin's hanging down, and your hair's falling out. What's goin on?" she asked with a strange look in her bloodshot eyes.

Just then, the big white Ram smashed into my side of the Caddy, and we all went flying, tumbling, turning, and rolling.

I woke up with sweat running down my face and my T- shirt soaking wet.

I must have yelled or something because Jeanie had a hold of my arm and was shaking me awake.

"I'm so sorry . . . had a bad dream," I said.

I hope this isn't the beginning of something I have to look forward to, I thought to myself.

After all the death and crime scenes that I've seen over my almost 50 years of police work, I had never had any bad dreams or unsettling thoughts, but I was afraid that the case involving Pea might just be the exception.

I took a long pull on a strong Crown Reserve, closed my eyes, and wondered,

Should I tell Jeanie that I'm a 77-year old man? Would she even believe me? What if she

woke up next to an old man some morning, then what? I really don't know what the hell to do at this point!

When I opened my eyes, she was sitting there just quietly watching me.

"Are you alright, hun?" she asked. "You look very troubled."

"I'm fine, but there's something I've been needing to tell you," and then I was silent for a few seconds while I tried to decide where to start.

"Yes, luv . . . what is it?"

"Ah . . . I'm not really sure how to say this; I'm not sure how you'll take it."

She looked at me intently,

"You can tell me anything. Have you got three wives at home or something like that?" and she smiled.

"Oh, hell no! Ok, here goes . . . you are the most beautiful woman I've ever known, and I think I'm falling in love with you."

There was silence.

"Is that it?" she asked.

"Well . . . yeah! Does some guy say that to you every day?"

"Which part . . . that I am beautiful or that he's falling in love?"

"Everything's a joke to you; I kind of like that in a lady," I said, and she stood and moved my way, sat down in my lap, put her amazing tongue in my mouth and halfway down my throat.

I wondered what kind of a joke she would come up with when I told her what was really on my mind, and I had to be friggin nuts!

You don't have any business falling for anyone at this point in time. Yer a fool, Chuck Benson, but I like her tongue, and she smells so good . . . and oh crap!

"What would you like for dinner, young lady?"

"Do you suppose they would deliver one of those amazing pizzas and a couple of bottles of wine?" she asked.

"Well, if they won't, it's just up the road; I'll go get it."

She put her hand in mine, and it was trembling.

"I really don't want to be left alone, babe."

"Don't worry about that. I'll find a way to get it here."

I called the pro shop and got Gary just as he was about to leave; I told him what we wanted, and he said,

"I'll have Bobby, the young assistant who watched yer camp the other day, pick it up and bring it to ya."

"That's great, Gary; thank you so much! I'll be leaving right after Jeff's memorial service on Friday just in case we don't hook up in all the confusion. I really can't thank you enough for all your hospitality!"

"No problem, Chuck! Anytime, my brother, just holler; we're doing the catering for Jeff's memorial, so I may be pretty busy as well, but we'll talk soon!"

I called Wilson and ran through the events of the last couple of days, and he decided that he'd fly in for the event.

"I'll see ya at the airport, buddy," I said, and the line went dead.

"You know, the pizza was growing on me, and the wine wasn't too bad either. Watson was doing a fairly decent job on his slice of pie, could have been the extra filet I ordered.

"What happened to the front end of yer pretty new SUV?" Wilson asked when I picked him up from the airport.

"Just a little altercation with an adobe wall and a locked door; nothin a little Bond-o and some paint won't fix."

He and Watson sat side-by-side in the back seat, and the pup put his right paw in Wilson's left hand, and the love affair was back on.

"Yer quite the boy, you are," Wilson said, and Watson barked.

Chapter 14

Jeff's memorial service was quite amazing to say the least. The only relatives who were in attendance were his two 50-something year-old kids who didn't really resemble him at all as both of them were kind of fat and sloppy-looking in jeans, T-shirts, and old boots. I suppose respect for the dead only ran so deep and figured they were just there for the money. I had no idea if Jeff even had any money to leave.

Every lady in town over the age of 65 showed up in her Sunday-best and glared at each other as if to say, "He liked me best." Jeff really was a rounder.

There was lots and lots of food, fresh-boiled shrimp and crab claws, prime rib, all kinds of salads, desserts, a keg of beer, and an open bar.

After an hour or so, some of the old gals were starting to get a little tipsy, and their sunbonnets began to tilt to one side, and I supposed a wig or two or more began to slide as well. One older lady came up to me and asked,

"Excuse me, are you Dr. Benson?"

"Yes, ma'am, I am," I said as I shook a gloved hand.

In her other hand was a large, clear, plastic cup that looked like it held straight whisky.

"Jeffy thought very highly of you," she said as she leaned forward and had to put her hand on my chest to keep her balance; she paused then squeezed,

"Oh, my, do you exercise?"

"I just do a little running from time to time."

"I used to have a personal trainer," she said, "But I finally had to let him go."

"I don't need a trainer; I need someone to follow me around and slap the crap out of me every time I try to put something in my mouth!" and she broke out laughing and spilled her drink; her wig and hat changed positions once again as she giggled.

I decided I needed to follow her lead,

"Point me towards the bar," I said, and I excused myself and headed toward Jeanie who was standing with Wilson and Watson.

They were all looking my way with a smile on their faces.

"Who's your friend, my luv?"

"Just one of Jeff's many concubines."

We dropped Wilson back at the airport to catch a 7:30 flight and then settled in back at camp for a couple of drinks and a good night's sleep.

We snuggled close, and Jeanie fell fast asleep. I had a few short dreams: one that included Pea and an old man fighting with knives, and one that included Jeanie and the same old man dancing on a golf green.

I awoke in the early morning and made a pot of joe. By the time Jeanie was dressed, it was ready; we sat at the small dinette table, looked into each other's eyes, and faked smiles,

"You wanna get something to eat?" I asked.

"No, thanks, luv. I really need to get on the road."

"Well, ok, then."

163

I loaded her large suitcase into the trunk of the brand-spanking new Chevy sedan.

It was a good thing I was young again or that damn suitcase would have had to stay there.

I told her I loved her then she gave me a long, sensual kiss, and just like that, she was gone.

Hey . . . wait . . . did she ever say she loved me? I don't think so. Well, damn! I guess that's the end of Ms. Jeanie Simms! We'll see.

I made the bed, readied the trailer for the road, and hooked up, and Watson and I were on to Phoenix for a speaking engagement and book signing that evening at 7:00pm.

We had been on the road for about 45 minutes when my phone rang, and I pushed the little phone thingy on the steering wheel,

"This is Chuck."

"Is this Dr. Chuck T. Benson?" a very sensual voice came over the speakers.

"Ah . . . yes it is . . . how can I help you?"

"I just wanted to say: *luv you, too!*"

Yes! I knew it, and I did a couple of fist pumps.

"So . . . ah . . . who is this again?' I asked.

"You are such an ass!" she said.

"Hey, I'm not the one who drove off without saying *I love you,* and further, I'm not the one who's dumb enough to fall in love with me," and there was silence on the line.

Finally, she spoke, "Where are you?"

"Just pulling into Phoenix, got a little shindig here this evening then off on a leisurely trip to Denver."

"Would you like some company in Denver?" she asked.

"Well . . . that depends on who it is,"

"Me, you jerk!"

"Oh, well . . . that wouldn't be so bad, I suppose."

"Chuck T. Benson, you are such an asshole, ya know?"

"Yeah, but I'm the asshole who saved yer beautiful neck and all yer other parts, for that matter."

"Yeppers! You sure did!" she said with a very sultry voice, "And I will be forever grateful."

"Are you doin ok?" I asked.

"Yes, I'm fine, just a little sore. I've got a couple more hours then I can rest in my own bed."

"Hey, Speedball Tucker, slow it down a little!"

165

"Who?" she asked.

"Never mind; it was before yer time."

She didn't know Glen Yarborough or Jim Croche? What the hell?

"Get some rest."

"Ok. Will you call me after your show?"

"It may be late."

"That's ok; I'm a night owl. I love you."

"See, was that so hard?" I said.

"No, asshole . . . as a matter of fact, it was very easy! Don't you have something to say to me in reply?"

I cringed, "You smell good wet."

"WHAT?"

"Uh, I mean . . . I love you, too."

I chastised myself,

Now look what you've started; maybe after a couple of months of long-distance romance she'll get tired of this game; or maybe, the old Chuck will come back, and she'll never find me again . . . OR . . . maybe the aliens who caused this problem in the first place will come down and just snatch me up. I know I'm a scientist, and I'm supposed to be able to figure things out, but right now, that sounds about as good as anything.

My editor had previously shipped four cases of my books to the gal who sponsored the event in Phoenix, and she had a table set up along with a couple of cuties from Arizona State University to hand me books and fight back all the screaming women who were ripping off pieces of clothing and throwing them in my direction . . . ah, wait . . . I may have just dozed off again.

At any rate, we sold all but a half a dozen books or so, and I gave them to my sponsor who in return, gave me kiss on the cheek that was a little more passionate than normal (I mean usually I don't have to wipe the saliva from my ear); she also gave me an envelope with $1,150 in cash; then she winked and asked me if I'd like a drink, so we could talk about next year's event.

"Well . . . usually I let my publisher handle these things, but . . ."

I'll be honest, I did want a drink, and she really was an attractive woman, and after all, I was just a big whore-dog. So, what's-her-name left the trailer about 1:15 with her T's crossed, I's dotted, her eyes properly crossed, and a very large smile on her face and not a minute too soon as my phone rang, OH, CRAP!

"Hey . . . ah . . . babe! How are you?"

"I thought you were gonna call me!" Jeanie said with a pout in her voice I could hear through the phone line.

"Absolutely, baby! I just walked in."

"Where were you all night? It's after 2:00am."

"Oh . . . it's barely after one here."

There was silence.

"Just a bunch of folks who wanted to visit and then get something to eat; actually, that's a lie," I said. "Four young ladies from the ASU cheerleading squad abducted me, and they all had their way with me, and I just escaped."

"You crazy bastard, you had me worried!"

"Sweetheart, I think you know that I can take care of myself. I'll talk to you tomorrow."

"Don't you want to talk to me, now?" she asked.

"I'm worn out, babe; let me call you when I'm on the road. Good night!" and I hung up.

At the other end of the line, Jeanie sat up in her bed with her mouth open,

Did that SOB just hang up on me?

Chapter 15

The next morning, Watson and I had fresh air in our lungs and the wind in our hair as we worked our way north and a little east toward Denver. It supposedly was only 800 miles, about 13 hours if people stayed out of our way. Watson barked with enjoyment as he stuck his face out the window.

Apparently, the people feeding information to my GPS didn't know crap because the faster I went, the further I seemed to get behind; it was either that, or Denver just kept moving to mess with me.

About four in the afternoon, I saw a sign that read *Good Sam Trailer Village* just ahead, and I ended up getting a space right by the swimming pool that had convenient water, electric, and sewer hookups.

After we set up camp, I put out the welcome mat, poured myself a cocktail, and broke out my guitar. The young ladies walking hither and yon all noticed Watson playing the guitar, and the heavy bandage around his shoulder just added to his allure. Before long, we had about eight or ten extremely attractive and fit young ladies with half-full cups and very skimpy bikinis sitting in a half-circle all around the front of us.

One particularly busty young lady asked if Watson was hungry.

"Are you hungry, boy?"

Two large barks, and she had the answer to that question. Come to find out, the group of young girls was part of a visiting college volleyball team, and they had just won the regional title and were in the mood to celebrate.

"Sweet cheeks" returned with a tray full of smoked brisket, sausage, and some rolls, and I broke out a very new and very large bottle of Crown Royal Reserve and set it on the grass in front of our audience.

As it turned out, the brisket lady and one other very nice-looking, twenty-something, bound on destroying her reputation, ended up staying the longest.

I wasn't really sure of the time, but it was late. I bid our guests a good night and left the nearly empty bottle on the lawn, and Watson and I went inside and left the trailer door wide open and the screen unlocked. I could hear them talking between themselves and giggling.

I stripped down to my altogether and slid between the cool sheets, and it couldn't have been four maybe five minutes later, that I heard the screen door open.

Watson jumped down and went to his bed in the dining area as almost simultaneously, two young, firm, naked bodies found their way into my bed,

"Dr. Benson . . . will you have one more drink with us?"

The next morning, the brisket lady and the blonde tornado, as I named her during the night for some reason I couldn't seem to recall, were gone. I walked outside and found the whole team was gone! The trailer park was empty except for me. Thank God! That was one less story I'd have to make up and remember.

Watson and I jumped into the pool then took a quick shower, packed up, and we were on the road again. Hopefully, it was only seven or so more hours to Denver, but the thought crossed my mind that we would just spend another night on the road,

"Whaddaya say to that, kiddo?" and he barked his agreement as I dialed Jeanie's number.

"Hello?" Jeanie answered her phone on the first ring.

"Hey, ladybug, how you doin this beautiful day? We stopped at a roadside park by a creek last evening and didn't have any phone service; we had a few cocktails, sang a few songs, and called it a night. I may lose ya cause we're goin through some purdy rugged country; if I do, I'll call ya back as soon as I get reception. What?"

"When are you" . . . static . . . static . . . static.

We went about 30 miles before we got any decent reception, and I called Jeanie back,

"Hey, kiddo!"

"What's up with you?"

"I'm driving; got to go up to Alamogordo and Ruidoso to check on a couple of stores."

"You are not over doing it, are ya, baby?"

"No, I'm fine, a little stiff is all."

"Ok. I'll see you in a few days, and I expect you to be the same."

"Very nice talk, girl, just calm down before you hurt yourself! Hey, sweetie, I'm pullin into Alamo. I gotta go. Talk to ya soon; I love . . ." and CLICK, she was gone.

Did she just hang up on me? Damn it!

We slipped back into Colorado somewhere around three, and I had a feeling we weren't gonna make it to big D (not Dallas) that night.

Five nights later, we were settled into a cozy little trailer park with a view of a small lake out our front door with absolutely NO excitement of any kind since we've arrived. It was restful and peaceful, but I was beginning to get that *itch*.

We spent the afternoon with no luck trying to find a vet clinic that would let me remove the staples from Watson's left shoulder, so I finally had to go into a "doc in the box" and show my credentials. They agreed to let me use their OR, and it took about five minutes for me to do what I needed to, then we were back on the road with my bank roll being $100 poorer. I guess it was worth it, though, as I'd pay any amount to keep Watson healthy, but a $100 for five minutes to me was a little much.

Watson walked around the front of the trailer for a short time then went down to the lake for a swim. When he returned, he was walking normal and seemed as good as new.

"Hey, kiddo, looks like yer doc did a purdy good job," and he came up to me, licked my face, and barked.

The next morning after a breakfast of burritos and hash browns at Mickey D's (Watson had scrambled eggs and bacon because he wasn't much for Mexican food); we wandered on over to the Civic Center to check out the venue. A nice, elderly lady at the office found a key and showed Watson and I to a smaller room that was off to the right side of the main hall,

"I'm not sure dogs are allowed in here, Mr. Benson!"

"I assure you its fine. He's Dr. Benson, and I'm just his manager."

She gave me a look that said, "I don't think that's very funny!"

The room looked like it would hold maybe 250 people, and I asked,

"What about the big room next door? He is purdy famous, you know."

"You'll have to talk to Ms. Rosen about that; she's in charge of your event this evening."

A few seconds later, a very pleasant voice from behind me rang out in the empty auditorium,

"Dr. Benson!"

I turned around, and a very attractive 30-something brunette in an expensive short-sleeve sweater and brown tweed skirt cut just above her knees, wearing brown, patent leather heels and sporting a tiny waist started to speak and then stopped in her tracks with a look of surprise on her face,

"Ah . . . Dr. Benson?"

"Yes, ma'am, I'm Chuck Benson, and who might you be?"

"Mable . . ." she said, "You can go back to your desk; I will handle this," and Mable gave me a look and walked away.

"You are not at all what I was expecting, Doctor . . . ah . . ."

"Oh, this?" and I held my hands toward my face. "I understand, just some maintenance in my off time . . . Miss . . . Mrs. . . . ah . . ."

"MISS Rosen, Jan Rosen," she said.

"Well, Ms. Rosen . . ."

"Oh, please, you can call me, Jan."

"Well, Jan, how we doing for tonight?" I asked.

"We only have a few seats left, and if we don't sell them this afternoon, we're sure to this evening at the door."

"Great . . . will you be here this evening?" I asked.

"Oh, yes, of course! I'll be introducing you and helping you at the table during the signing."

"Wonderful!" I said, "And, I suppose my books made it here?"

"Oh, yes! I have four cases in my office."

At that point, Watson came up behind her and touched her butt with his nose, and she jumped in shock.

"Watson, stop! I am sorry about that!"

"It's fine, just caught me by surprise," and she bent down on one knee, and they exchanged kisses.

"What a beautiful dog! What is he?"

"Labrador and poodle mix," I said.

"What happened here?" she asked as she ran her hand carefully over the shaved area around his scar.

"A little altercation with a mad man down in Tucson a week or so ago."

She looked at me once more and held her glance,

"You are *that* Chuck Benson?"

"Guilty as charged," I said.

"Wow! The manager of the center and I are just about to go to lunch; would you care to join us?"

"Sure; why not."

At lunch, my new friends and I sat and conversed for an hour or more; then it was time for me to get back to the trailer and take Watson his corned beef sandwich and prepare for the evening.

The event was going to be nothing major, just basically a short talk with a meet-n-greet afterwards, probably would only have a couple of cocktails while I signed some books.

Back at my trailer, I sprayed some starch on a pair of Wranglers and a white shirt and ironed some creases into them. I checked my black tweed, western sportscoat and made sure there were no surprises as I hadn't worn it since Sheriff Jeff's memorial, made sure my boots had a good coat of polish and a shine on them, and well, that was about it.

I sat in a lawn chair in the cool, spring air and dozed off. When I awoke, it was around six in the evening, so I dressed and put a little *smellem-good* on, and Watson and I started out the door. Just before I got to the truck, my phone rang,

"Watson . . . go do yer business, kiddo! This is Chuck..."

"Hey, baby . . . how ya doin?"

"Hey, Jeanie, how are you, gal?"

"Fine. I'm about two hours away."

I gave her the address of the trailer park, told her the key was between the tires and to let herself in and that I would leave word at the door to let her in if she wanted to come on over to the Convention Center.

It was 6:30 by the time I got to the Center, and Jan had some large posters placed on easels outside both sets of double doors. Inside, there were streamers and tiny lights strung on wire all over the room, looked really nice, not quite what I was expecting.

Jan was attending the table, setting my books out in stacks, and she had what looked to be an extremely cute, high school girl in jeans and a lacy top with her hair up in pigtails assisting her,

"What's the occasion?" I asked.

"Oh . . . just some old writer trying to sell some books," she replied with a smile. "Chuck, this is my daughter, Risa."

She shook my hand and smiled.

I said, "Aren't you a pretty one?" and she smiled, blushed, and whispered,

"Thank you."

Glenna Russell was walking around in the foyer of the Civic Center trying to formulate a plan; the big bag that hung across her shoulder made of burlap was not completely out of place, but it definitely didn't match her outfit.

She was only 57 years old, but she looked and felt much older, probably because of all the loss she had endured in her life. Her daughter was probably in a crack house somewhere between there and California, maybe even dead, and she hadn't heard from her in over a year. Her husband, the only man she had ever loved, died of cancer a year or so ago, and the knowledge that her Mark was gone forever made a tear come to her eye as she sipped her sweet rose wine from the cheap plastic glass they had given her at the bar.

She took another big swallow of her wine, emptying her glass. She checked her watch: it was 7:20, and she figured she had time to have another drink, so she made her way back over to the bar.

"Is this the only size glass you have?" and she showed the empty glass to the young, pimple-faced girl behind the service counter.

"Yes, ma'am. I'm so sorry! The city won't let us sell any larger than that; there's a code or something."

"Well . . . hell!" Glenna was perturbed, "Give me two, then!"

The young girl smiled as she filled the first glass and set it in front of Glenna. She took the glass, held it up, looked at it, then downed it in two swallows and set the glass back on the counter.

"Better make it three!"

The young girl just smiled and poured one more.

"That'll be $24, ma'am."

Glenna dug down deep into her big bag and found her wallet; she pulled out $30 and tossed it on the counter.

"Keep the change, dearie!"

"Oh, thank you, ma'am!" but Glenna didn't turn around. She just walked into the almost-full auditorium and took a seat in the back.

She looked at her watch. The numbers looked blurry, but she determined it was 7:29, and she took another swallow of her pink wine.

A pretty, young lady snuck in and sat next to her just as Jan Rosen walked on stage, and the house lights went down.

"Good evening, ladies and gentlemen. I'm Jan Rosen, Assistant Director of the Special Event Civic Center, and it's my pleasure to introduce to you all this evening, Dr. Chuck T. Benson and his companion, Watson," and she held her right hand toward the side of the stage, and we walked out. We kissed each other on the cheek, and she handed me the microphone.

I walked out to the center of the stage, told Watson to *heel*, then *stay*, and he took his place by my right side.

"Watson . . . can you say *howdy* to the nice folks?" and he barked so the whole arena could hear, eliciting our first round of applause. It didn't take me long to learn that as long as Watson was on the stage, people didn't care what I talked about.

"How y'all doin this evening?" I went through my canned spiel like I had a 100 or more times before.

In the back of the room, Glenna took another gulp and emptied her plastic wine-glass. She held it up, looked right then left, then let it fall to the concrete floor, causing a rattling sound throughout the small area. Many people looked her way, but she just looked up with a half-smile on her face and wondered where the man on the poster was, the man who had killed her Markey.

She was very confused; the young man talking on stage didn't resemble the old man on the poster, and the woman sitting beside her seemed very confused as well. Jeanie had gone to my webpage that had my latest picture on it and had read my story; nothing seemed to match, which made no sense to her.

Forty minutes later . . .

"And, so, in closing, I'd like to tell you a story about two friends of mine from over around San Antone, two brothers, Poncho and Pedro. They were both very hard working Mexican men, good men, but one day, Pedro got kicked by a mule, which crippled him, causing him to have to walk with crutches. The two boys had a terrible time trying to survive.

Each week Poncho would come into town to buy what supplies they could afford, and he would see the priest, and the holy father would ask,

"Poncho, how is your brother, Pedro?"

"Oh, *Padre*, he's cripple, you know?"

"Yes, I know . . . tell him that I'm praying for him." and this went on for many years until one day, around Christmas time, Poncho was in town for supplies, and the priest saw him and asked,

"Poncho, how is your brother, Pedro?"

Poncho replied, "Oh, *Padre,* the most wonderful thing happened: yesterday we were at your church, and Pedro wanted to pray. He put some holy water on his left leg, and he threw that crush away."

The preacher's eyes opened wide, and he listened more intently,

"Yes . . . my son . . . what happen then?"

"Well, then he rubbed some holy water on his right leg, and he threw his other crush away."

The priest got all excited and exclaimed,

"Praise God, and he walked, yes?"

Poncho said,

"Oh, HELL no! He fall on his ass . . . he's cripple, you know?"

183

Silence, then laughter and applause.

"Good night and thank y'all for coming; for those of you who are interested, Watson and I will be signing books at this table right down here. Say *good night*, Watson..." and he barked out loud.

I left the stage and grabbed a bottle of water. Then I went down front and took a seat. The line was long, and people were smiling and having an enjoyable time.

"Thank you! I'm glad you enjoyed it! Yes, ma'am, $20 dollars. You can pay the pretty lady to your left."

I sold books and talked to people for an hour or so; the atmosphere in the room was very high and light, and everybody seemed to be having a good time.

The line was down to the last half a dozen people when an older lady in a floral dress that had seen better days stood in front of me at the table; her grey hair was up in a bun, and she carried a bag that would hold several of each one of my books.

"How are you tonight, my dear?" I asked.

"Are you the Dr. Benson who killed Mark Russell?"

I was quiet for a few seconds,

"Ah, yes, ma'am, that was me."

She reached down in her big bag and pulled out a shiny hatchet, and the light from the blade reflected into my eyes, so much so, that I was blinded for a second or two. Then I heard a loud scream,

"CHUCK . . . LOOK OUT!"

The old lady turned her back to me. Jeanie ran towards her, and with one, smooth stroke Glenna cut Jeanie's neck from ear to ear, causing her to collapse to the floor.

Watson, sleeping at my feet reacted: he jumped and hit Glenna in the chest, knocking her to the ground. He locked his big mouth around her throat, bit down, and growled as he rode the body of Glenna Russell to the concrete floor. He straddled her until I told him to *heel*, but by then, it was too late.

Jeanie was lying there, unmoving, in a pool of her own blood. Glenna just laid there on the floor trying to breathe from the wound she had sustained from Watson's sharp teeth; the hatchet laid by her side, covered in blood.

I ran over to Jeanie and checked for a pulse, but she was gone.

The next day, I sat in Jan Rosen's office, and it was a very somber occasion. She gave me an envelope with $2,200 cash and asked me where I was headed. I just shook my head as I really didn't know.

"You are welcome to stay around here. I have a large house that can accommodate both you and Watson."

I said, "I appreciate the kind offer; maybe next time."

Watson and I made our way back to our campsite, readied the trailer for travel, and pulled out onto the highway. It was still early, and the sun shone bright in the cloudless sky.

Losing Jeanie somehow took all the fun out of the moment, and to what purpose? I sat up straight in the seat of the caddy and asked Watson,

"So where to now, kiddo?"

He just kinda moaned as if to reply,

"I'd say *home*, but this is it!"

We left Denver and headed south.

All of a sudden, my bones felt heavy, and I felt really . . . old. Watson looked my way and gave me a high-pitched moan,

"What?"

He moaned again, and I looked at myself in the rearview,

"AH CRAP!"

THE END!

OTHER BOOKS BY DUKE CHARLES

LUKE KASH WESTERN SERIES:

People of the Horse
Spirit and the Blood
Blood and Thunder
Thunder Cloud and Spirit Walker
The Spirit Rides With Me

ROC REESE SERIES:

Birdies and San Diego Heat
Birdies and Vegas Heat
Birdies and Texas Riviera Heat
Birdies and New Orleans Heat
Birdies and Maui Heat

LEE LOVELADY SERIES:

A Texas Melody
The Texas Two-Step

OTHER BOOKS BY DUKE CHARLES:

Blanco River Wars
Black Wolf Moon
From Hell to Kingsville
Fire on the Water

All books by Duke Charles are
available in print
and digitally at

DukeCharles.com

You can also find them at
Amazon.com,
Barnes&Noble.com,

and everywhere great fiction
is sold.

For book signings and speaking engagements, contact Duke

at

DukeCharlesWriter@gmail.com

Like Duke on Facebook

Follow Duke on LinkedIn